The
REAWAKENING

Ann Evans

USBORNE

Thank heavens for sons who understand computers!
For you, Wayne, for unravelling my IT dilemmas
time and again.
Love also to Mel, Megan and the new arrival...

This edition first published in the UK in 2007 by Usborne Publishing Ltd.,
Usborne House, 83-85 Saffron Hill, London EC1N 8RT, England.
www.usborne.com

First published in 2007. Text copyright © Ann Evans, 2007.
Cover copyright © Usborne Publishing Ltd., 2007.

A CIP catalogue record for this book is available from the British Library.

JFMA JJASOND/07 ISBN 9780746078822 Printed in Great Britain.

The Midland Daily Chronicle

HOLIDAYMAKERS are warned to be on their guard following stories that the ghost of a prehistoric animal has been sighted in a remote Scottish valley.

Reports state that the spirit of a sabre-toothed tiger is roaming Endrith Valley – nicknamed Valley of Shadows because of the legendary ghostly sightings of Highland warriors who fought a ferocious battle there 700 years ago.

The ghostly tiger has supposedly attacked two young holidaymakers – brother and sister, Grant and Amanda Laird, aged 14 and 12 respectively, of Wolverton in the West Midlands. They say that they encountered the beast while holidaying with their parents in August of this year.

"It was terrifying," said red-haired Amanda, a pupil of Wolverton Comprehensive. "It stalked us, gradually manifesting itself until you could see it clearly. It was huge, with massive fangs and claws. My brother and I had to run for our lives. It wanted to kill us."

The youngsters' parents, however, experienced none of these supernatural events and Mrs. Connie Laird commented that she thought her children were suffering from sunstroke at the time.

FACT FILE

- Sabre-toothed tigers became extinct 10,000 years ago.
- They were about the size of a lion, but heavier.
- As carnivores they probably used stealth and ambush rather than speed to catch their prey.
- Their sabre teeth would have been used to puncture the soft underbelly of their prey.

chapter one

With the golden-brown puppy secure in his arms, thirteen-year-old Daniel Glenn joined Beth and the others in the ghostbusting van.

Not that the grown-ups liked any of their stuff being referred to as *ghostbusting* – especially Melissa. Melissa was secretary of the ghostbusting team – or rather the Psychic Study Society. And this wasn't a ghostbusting van at all. It was a specially converted Volkswagen Transporter, equipped with all the latest mobile psychic-phenomena-detecting equipment, with seating for five passengers and one puppy named Scooby.

Daniel turned briefly and waggled the puppy's paw in the direction of his mum, who was standing at the front door waiting to wave goodbye to him, his dad and the others.

Dad was Andrew Glenn, Chairman of the Psychic Study Society – or PSS – and he was in the front seat next to Melissa. She was squeezed next to Len Moran, driver-owner of the ghostbusting van. Len's normal job, when he wasn't chasing ghosts, was as a builder. He was a big, muscled guy who didn't look the sort to believe in ghosts at all. Although actually, neither did Daniel's dad, who was a police sergeant in his day job.

Melissa looked batty enough though. Melissa Iona Isis, if that was her real name. Daniel thought she'd probably made it up to go with her profession as a herbalist and ghostbuster.

Len put the van into gear and everyone waved to Daniel's mum as they set off for the Highlands of Scotland in search of a ghostly sabre-toothed tiger and some ancient battling warriors. At least that was the grown-ups' reason for this trip. As for Daniel, it was a great way to spend a week of the summer holiday. He and Scooby were going to have a fantastic time.

Len's daughter, Beth, had come along for the trip too. She'd just had her eleventh birthday and was starting at Daniel's school in September. Her eyes lit up at the sight of the puppy.

"Oh! How gorgeous. What's its name?"

"Scooby. She's only four months old and already sits and gives you her paw...you're a clever girl, aren't you, Scooby?"

After licking Daniel on the nose, the puppy decided to investigate the other passengers and nuzzled excitedly into Melissa's mop of tousled grey-black hair, possibly in search of a dangly earring. Daniel dragged her back, easing strands of hair from the pup's mouth as Melissa's face screwed itself up in pain.

"Sorry, she's just a bit excited," Daniel apologized.

"A puppy!" Melissa wailed, throwing her hands up in despair so that all her bracelets tinkled and the rings on her fingers caught the sunlight. "Andrew, it's hardly a good idea bringing a puppy with us! It's going to be so distracting."

Andrew Glenn spoke with his usual calm authoritative voice – his policeman's voice, was how Daniel's mum jokingly described it. "She'll be fine. She'll keep the kids occupied. Besides, it's good for them all to get some fresh air and exercise."

Melissa looked unconvinced. "And *children* too! Andrew, I told you I had reservations about bringing children along. I'm still concerned that they'll create too much of a disturbance. Children aren't renowned for keeping quiet or still."

"The kids will be fine," Andrew assured her. "They've promised to be on their best behaviour." He cast a warning glance over his shoulder. "Haven't you, Daniel?"

"Of course!" Daniel exclaimed innocently. "I'm going to be busy training Scooby anyway. I'll be teaching her to fetch, and come and stay—"

"Yes, stay well out of the way," Melissa interrupted. "This is a serious field trip. I intend to write an article for the national psychic press about our findings. We need to be fully concentrated on this expedition."

Behind her back, Daniel did an impression of Melissa's stern expression, making Beth giggle. Melissa took her ghostbusting activities very seriously. She was "very sensitive to supernatural phenomena", or so he'd overheard his dad telling Mum one day. Daniel thought she was just peculiar.

"I see our field trip plans made last night's *Gazette*, folks," Andrew remarked, showing Melissa a newspaper cutting. "It's actually not a bad write-up. For once we haven't been made to sound like a bunch of crackpots. Although the press have picked up on the sabre-toothed tiger angle, rather than the main reason we're going."

"Well, we knew they would," said Len. "Sabre-toothed tigers coming back to life is slightly more sensational than ghostly battle sounds being heard." With a wry smile on his face he steered the van out onto the main road and headed along the northbound highway. "Anyway, what have they said?"

"I'll read it, shall I?" Melissa suggested, adjusting her purple-tinted spectacles. "Now, let's see... A group of ghost hunters—" She instantly tutted. "How I detest that expression. Andrew, I thought you said the article didn't make us sound like crackpots!"

"Just read it, Melissa," grinned Len.

She tutted again before continuing. "A group of...*ghost hunters* are heading for the Highlands of Scotland in search of a prehistoric beast thought to be roaming a Scottish valley. The Psychic Study Society is planning a field trip to coincide with the date that two ancient Highland clans fought a bloody battle in 1314.

"It was around this particular time last year that the beast, described as the ghost of a prehistoric sabre-toothed tiger, was reported to have stalked and attacked two children camping with their parents.

"Andrew Glenn, chairman of the PSS, said – and I'm quoting you now, Andrew – 'This valley is reputed to be haunted. The sounds of a battle have been reported on numerous occasions. Regarding the beast incident, I have interviewed the children involved and found their account of the whole event to be most convincing. We are intrigued by their encounter, and while it does seem highly unlikely that a prehistoric ghost could still be around, we are going in with open minds.'" Melissa glanced up from the newspaper cutting. "End quote!"

Beth leaned towards her dad. "It didn't actually *hurt* those children, did it? I mean, it couldn't, could it? It was a ghost..."

"Of course not!" Len laughed. "We'd hardly be bringing you kids if there was any danger, would we?"

"I'll read on, shall I?" Melissa interrupted. "Now, where was I? Ah yes! Members of the Psychic Study Society, which was founded six years ago, range from doctors to engineers. Three of them will be setting off fully equipped with the latest ghostbusting devices such as electromagnetic field detection meters, infrared motion sensors and ion detectors, which measure disturbance in the air when spirit energy is present. Mr. Glenn, who is a police sergeant in his day job, added – another quote from you, Andrew – 'We have state of the art technology behind us. If there is anything supernatural hanging around the Valley of Shadows, then believe me we will find it.'"

Melissa folded the newspaper cutting and passed it back to Andrew. "It's quite exciting, isn't it? You know, I have a distinct feeling that this trip is going to produce some very interesting findings."

"So you think we might really see a ghost when we get to Scotland?" Beth asked quietly, fiddling with her long blonde ponytail.

"Spirit, dear, not ghost," Melissa corrected her. "Spirit entities. A ghost is only able to repeat an action over and over again, like a video player replaying itself. Whereas a spirit has the ability to progress, to interact, to make contact with living beings, to manifest itself even."

"What does manifest mean?" Beth asked, looking puzzled.

"Become real," Melissa announced, taking another newspaper cutting from her embroidered shoulder bag. "If you read this original report, those Laird children say that the spirit of this beast gradually manifested itself and tried to kill them."

"Kill them!" Beth gasped, making the puppy dive for cover under Daniel's armpit. "I thought you said a ghost can't hurt you?"

"It can't!" stated Len, casting Melissa a stern glance. "And I think you'd better stop scaring the kids, Melissa, or they'll be having nightmares."

"I'm only repeating what we've been told. Andrew's the one who went off and interviewed the Laird children – and you believed them, didn't you? Besides, our life force is energy," she went on, giving Andrew no chance to speak. "Energy is neither created nor destroyed. It's simply transferred from place to place or from one form to another."

Beth's eyes were like saucers. "So we might actually *see* a sabre-toothed tiger – in real life...or death, rather?"

"Wouldn't *that* be incredible?" Melissa

sighed, turning in her seat, sending a waft of herby, flowery scent all through the van. For a second the sunlight glinting through the window caught her spectacles, making her eyes look wild and excited.

"Steady on now," Andrew Glenn said calmly. "Let's not let our imaginations run away with us. We're simply going to collect data which might indicate the presence of such a spirit. We'll weigh up our findings and make our judgements from that. Personally, I don't hold out much hope of finding evidence of something that lived ten thousand years ago – it's interesting, though, and those Laird children seemed level-headed enough. I don't *think* they were lying. They experienced some kind of phenomenon, I'm sure, though it's very unlikely they actually saw a sabre-toothed tiger. I think any paranormal experience was probably linked with the battle."

Beth clutched her dad's shoulder. "But what if they were telling the truth? What if the tiger is real? What if it manifests itself and comes after *us*?"

"Nothing is going to hurt you, Beth," Len said, patting her hand reassuringly. "We won't be fighting off prehistoric wild animals, I promise! We'll just be noting temperature changes, electromagnetic disturbances, that sort of thing, which may or may not indicate some paranormal goings-on. No different from what we usually do. And we haven't been chased by a ghost yet!"

Melissa seemed oblivious to the fact that she was worrying Beth, and gushed excitedly on. "But don't forget we'll be camping directly where the Battle of Endrith took place seven hundred years ago – on the very anniversary, no less! Mysterious sounds have been heard on many occasions; it's well documented."

Daniel glanced at Beth. She already looked like she'd seen a ghost. "It's all rubbish," he whispered, placing Scooby on her lap to take her mind off all this paranormal stuff. "I've read that newspaper article and I reckon those kids were making it all up."

Beth didn't look too convinced. "I don't mind ghostly sounds," she murmured, stroking Scooby so vigorously that the puppy was practically splayed flat on her lap. "It's the thought of something trying to *kill* us that scares me."

"It's not real!" Daniel groaned. "Even my mum thinks it's rubbish. She says the only reason she doesn't mind Dad being involved in all this is because it's a break from the stress of being a police sergeant."

"But my dad believes in ghosts," hissed Beth. "Or he wouldn't waste his time doing this. So ghosts *must* be real."

"Of course they are real!" Melissa interrupted, overhearing them. "And this spirit of an animal absolutely intrigues me. Those Laird children actually *saw* it. They were able to describe its colour and markings and its size. Just imagine how fantastic it would be if we could catch it on camera or video. It would give our group such an important standing in the world of paranormal investigation."

Daniel shook his head. The story was a hoax. Those Laird kids had invented the whole thing just to get their names in the paper. Ghosts were stupid.

Figments of people's imaginations – even intelligent and sensible people, like his dad and Len. It was just their hobby, like some people collected stamps. Their dads investigated the paranormal. They were always off to some haunted house or other, looking for paranormal evidence. All his dad ever came back with was weird photos of empty rooms, with maybe the occasional glow of light, or sometimes recordings of strange noises like electrical interference. No see-through figures wailing and clinking their chains.

And certainly no ghostly sabre-toothed tigers.

The mid-August sunshine glinting through the windows, coupled with the monotonous drone of the van's engine, eventually made the passengers sleepy. Heads lolled dozily as the landscape flashed by.

Gradually the skyline changed, as jagged mountain peaks crept over the horizon. The multi-colours of towns faded into great expanses of browns, purples and greens. Hills grew larger and more impressive at every twist and turn in the road. Valleys became deeper, more lush and sweeping. Woodland turned into forests, studded with exquisite shimmering lochs. By late afternoon the ghostbusting van with its passengers and paranormal equipment seemed like a dinky toy surrounded and overshadowed by towering mountains.

"Welcome to the Highlands of bonnie Scotland!" Len announced, changing down a gear to manoeuvre around a sharp bend.

Daniel opened heavy eyes and his stomach lurched. The land alongside the road seemed to have slipped steeply away so that treetops were practically at eye level as they followed the curve in the road. "Oh, wow! That's some view!" he exclaimed.

Beth sat up suddenly. "Don't go too fast, Dad," she fretted, leaning forward and holding on to his shoulder.

"No problem, love," Len said cheerfully. "Now keep your eyes peeled, folks. Any time now, there should be a signpost to Endrith Valley."

"Endrith!" Melissa spluttered, waking suddenly. "Are we there yet?"

Andrew exploded into laughter. "Funny, I was expecting the kids to be asking 'Are we nearly there yet?', not you, Melissa!"

"Just getting my bearings," she remarked dryly.

The road to Endrith Valley turned out to be a narrow single-tracked lane, which threaded its way around gigantic mountains like a slender golden ribbon, while ahead, shadows lengthened.

Changing up and down the gears, Len climbed hillsides so high that everyone's ears popped, and then swept down into picturesque valleys where rushing streams cascaded over rocks, and white frothing waterfalls caught the late afternoon sunlight, creating tiny rainbows.

"I've heard they're building a dual carriageway through here next year," Len remarked, glancing across a meadow. "It'll be a shame to cut up the landscape."

"That's progress, I guess," Andrew mused as he studied the map. "Okay, now somewhere along here we turn left..."

Endrith Valley finally emerged, and everyone, even Scooby, sat bolt upright to take in the view.

A sweeping green, grassy valley spread out spectacularly before them. It was bordered on the right by a dense forest of tall pine and gleaming silver birch trees, while to the left towered a mountain – imposing and majestic. And between the two lay a great expanse of grey-blue water that sparkled and shimmered beneath the pale sunlight.

Daniel's eyes were drawn towards the mountain that dominated the valley. Its lower slopes were grassy, but higher up it turned into pure grey granite, pitted with caves and ridges. Its peak was white, dusted with snow. It stood defiantly – as it had since time began.

"The Valley of Shadows!" Melissa breathed.

And for no apparent reason, Scooby started to whimper.

chapter two

"What's wrong with Scooby, Daniel?" Beth murmured, fussing the pup, who seemed really agitated.

"Dunno! What's up, matey?"

Melissa turned in her seat and stared at the dog. There was an odd glint in her eye. "It's perfectly obvious what's wrong with the dog. Canines are often susceptible to the paranormal.

She's probably already picked up on mystic vibes."

Beth's eyes widened. "The sabre-toothed tiger, you mean?"

"No!" Len cut in before Melissa could say anything more. "She probably just needs the toilet. So, let's get parked up and let her out!"

They set up camp in the heart of the valley – Daniel and his dad in one tent, Beth and her dad in another. Melissa had a large frame tent that they all had to help erect.

Before they'd even finished pegging it down, Melissa was inside setting up the ghostbusting equipment – laptop computers, a thermal-imaging camera, two night-vision camcorders, motion detectors and an assortment of hand-held monitors. Finally she hung strings of crystals and stones from the tent poles.

Once the gas barbecue and Primus stove were set up, Len rustled up a hot meal and drinks for everyone while Scooby gambolled in the grass and barked excitedly, happy now that she could stretch her little legs.

The evening was still warm, and the sun, gradually sinking towards the loch, turned the water a spectacular blood-red and gold. Everyone was relaxed. Only Melissa seemed in a hurry to start working.

"We need to check out all the places where reported sightings have occurred," she announced between hurried bites of chargrilled sausages. She had a hand-drawn map laid over her lap, marked with points of reference such as the *Laird family's camp...battle sounds heard...the beast first sighted...children chased by the beast.*

Suddenly, she became very still – frozen almost, except for her eyes, which darted this way and that behind her tinted spectacles. Finally she spoke, but her voice was so soft and hushed that a shiver ran unexpectedly down Daniel's spine. "It's here...can't you sense it? Can't you feel the power of its eternal spirit all around us?"

Daniel felt a gurgle of nervous laughter jump into his throat. In fact he wanted to laugh out loud. *Eternal spirits*...what a load of rubbish! But he spotted the look on his dad's face warning him *not* to take the mickey. So he bit his lip as Melissa floated off with the fairies.

"Its spirit prevails...I sense it... We are in a vortex of spiritual energy." She swayed gently as she spoke.

Beth's face creased into one big frown. "If you can sense *it*, won't it sense *us*? Won't it know that we're here, looking for it?"

"One can only hope," Melissa murmured, gazing mistily off into the distance.

"But what if it comes after us?" Beth fretted, inching closer to her dad. "What if it doesn't like people being here? Dad, what if—"

Len gave her a hug. "Stop worrying, love. There's nothing here to harm us. Nothing – I promise!"

After dinner, Daniel and Beth were appointed chief dish-washers, although Daniel found it more fun to flick soapsuds at Scooby, making her bark.

Melissa emerged from her tent loaded with ghost-hunting equipment. She glared disapprovingly. "Please try to stop that dog from barking incessantly. It's going to disturb all supernatural presences."

Without waiting for a reply, she strode off,

still grumbling that bringing children and animals was a bad idea. The two dads fell into line behind her, like soldiers following their sergeant major.

"We won't be long, kids," Andrew called back. "Just checking out a few localities."

As soon as they'd gone, Beth joined in flicking bubbles at Scooby. "You bark as much as you want. We don't want nasty dead sabre-toothed tigers hanging around here anyway."

"Melissa's nuts!" Daniel declared, stacking up the clean plates. "She's completely off her head if she thinks some prehistoric sabre-toothed tiger is going to stroll into our camp and pose for a photo!"

"So long as it doesn't stroll in and try to gobble us up!"

It was obvious that Beth was really bugged by this ghost thing. So Daniel decided to take her mind off it – by flicking soapsuds at *her*.

She retaliated by splashing him back and shrieked with laughter as a stream of washing-up water trickled off his nose.

Daniel responded with a handful of suds, sending Scooby into yaps of riotous barking – disturbing nothing except a large grey hare that had ventured close, unseen by anyone until it suddenly shot away towards the forest.

And one other entity that shifted in repose...

High on a mountain ridge overlooking the Valley of Shadows, a presence stirred. Karbel stretched out his spirit form, disturbing neither a speck of dust nor the tiniest of pebbles.

This huge beast, who had roamed the valley in prehistoric times, now rested here, deep between the layers of reality and eternity. Slumbering, contentedly. Requiring nothing from this earth except to remain in this place, in his domain for ever.

But his peace was briefly disturbed. And like a sleeping cat might flick a tail or whisker at an irritating fly, he moved restlessly in his long sleep. Momentarily, long razor-sharp claws extended from his massive paws. They stretched, as if exercising themselves, and then slowly retracted.

Something was interrupting his eternal rest. It was like the annoying buzz of an insect, only this was not a buzz, but a bark.

The high-pitched bark of a cub.

Deep in the furthest recesses of Karbel's memories, something stirred. But with a flick of his tail, he slept on. Sounds and sights and smells of this world no longer bothered him.

Karbel's mortal life had been over for thousands of years. Only briefly and rarely would he summon up the energy he needed to return to the world he had inhabited eons ago. And only then, if he had dreamed too long of hunting, and succumbed to the overpowering desire for the excitement of stalking his prey, and that moment of attack followed by the ripping and devouring of warm flesh.

Or like the last time, when he had feared his killer had returned. Then he had recognized the young male that entered his valley as the same human who had ended his mortal life so many centuries ago...

Then, he'd had no choice but to manifest himself. The effort left him drained. And eventually the human had left without harming his spirit. Since then other humans came and went from his valley without disturbing him.

Little bothered him now. Little disturbed his eternal rest.

The last rays of the sun were casting brilliant orange and silver streaks across a deep blue sky, reflecting a myriad of colours over the loch's surface.

With Scooby at their heels, Daniel and Beth wandered down to the water's edge, where bulrushes grew waist high. The loch shimmered, glinting and dazzling so that movement constantly caught the eye, making it seem as if something was out there.

"I wonder how deep it is," Beth remarked, trailing her hand through the tall reeds.

"Actually, I know the answer to that," grinned Daniel. "I was reading about it the other day. It's

250 metres deep in places – and that's *deep*!"

Beth shielded her eyes as she gazed across the water. "Plenty of room for a sea monster then?"

"Yeah, but this isn't Loch Ness," Daniel reminded her. "And I've never heard of the Loch Endrith monster! Hasn't quite got the same ring to it."

"No, Endrith just has its very own resident ghosts... Oh! What's that?" She jumped away from the water's edge.

"Jittery, aren't you!" Daniel laughed, peering out across the loch, seeing nothing except ripples.

Beth edged closer to him, practically hanging on to his arm. "I thought I saw something moving in the water. Look, over there..."

Daniel peered again, squinting against the glow of evening light. The entire surface of the loch was rippling, gently moving, swaying, as if something was causing a disturbance...as if something was swimming out there...swimming towards them.

The hairs on the back of his neck started to prickle. Something *could* be out there, just below the surface. Something big, judging by the way the whole surface rippled.

A monster! A relic from the past, from prehistoric times...like the Loch Ness monster.

Or the beast...

Beth was staring at him – and his imagination was running wild! Determinedly, he picked up a chunk of wood and hurled it as far out into the loch as he could. "Stop worrying, it's just the breeze."

The splash made Scooby yap, and the little pup pranced around the shoreline, barking excitedly at the advancing ripples.

"I'm sure I saw something!" Beth fretted, keeping well back from the water.

"You probably saw a fish jumping. Actually, my dad's brought his rods so he can go fishing if Melissa gives him time off for good behaviour. We've brought a little dinghy, too. We could try it out – unless you're too chicken to go out on the water!"

She shot him a defiant look. "I'm not chicken!"

He grinned. "Good! It'll be fun."

They strolled on, keeping well away from the

adults so they didn't disturb any of Melissa's *supernatural presences*. Scooby scampered on ahead, splashing in the shallow water, sniffing around in the bulrushes, getting muddier by the minute.

The silence of the valley was acute – unreal almost. Only Scooby's occasional bark shattered the quiet, and the sound echoed eerily across the valley.

Endrith Mountain towered straight ahead of them, its snowy peak darkening to grey as day drew to a close. Daniel gazed up at the craggy facade as he and Beth ambled on. Its ruggedness made perfect nesting places for birds of prey and... *ghostly sabre-toothed tigers.*

His stomach lurched. Now, where had *that* idea sprung from? And worse, he couldn't shake the thought from his head.

"You're quiet. What's up?" Beth eventually asked.

"Nothing. I'm just impressed by it all really," he fibbed. There was no point in telling Beth what he'd really been thinking. She was nervy enough.

Besides, it was a stupid thought anyway.

High above, a hawk circled, lifted by the warm currents to glide through the air before swooping down to land on a rocky platform and disappear from sight.

"I know what you mean." Beth sighed. "It's so beautiful here. It's odd to think that centuries ago it was a battlefield, with clans fighting each other. It's stupid really. Couldn't they have just all lived together in peace in such a beautiful country?"

"Yeah! Crazy, weren't they?" Daniel agreed, struggling to shake off his weird foreboding by throwing a tennis ball for Scooby. He couldn't believe it when his little dog chased it and actually brought it back. "Hey! Good girl, Scooby!"

Beth threw it next time, although it didn't go so far. As they watched the pup scamper after it, she said, "My dad was telling me that hundreds of Highlanders died in the Battle of Endrith Valley. They fought at dawn and when day finally broke hardly anyone was left alive. And it was here... right here in this valley – in this lovely quiet valley."

Daniel glanced at her. She was looking a bit too thoughtful again. "Hey! Don't go all weird on me like mad Melissa or I'll have to chuck you in the loch." And with a grin, he pretended he was going to do just that.

It did the trick, and shrieking loudly, Beth raced off with Daniel chasing after her and Scooby hot on their heels, yapping excitedly.

The barking, yapping sounds echoed across the valley and were lifted up on the breeze to a mountainous ridge. There, high above the valley, invisible to the human eye, a mighty creature stirred once more in sleep.

A tail twitched, as if swatting an annoying fly...and a tiny pebble shot off the ledge, as if blown away by a strong breeze.

"Well, chaps, what have we got?" Melissa Iona Isis asked, as everyone gathered beneath her tent awning to study their monitors and detectors.

Lamps dangled from the tent poles, and moths of all shapes and sizes fluttered madly around the orange glow.

"There's nothing unusual at all," Andrew stated, flicking through his notebook, as if reporting on a crime. "At nine o'clock the temperature was 12 degrees, electromagnetic fields perfectly normal. Ten o'clock saw the temperature fall by one degree. All pretty normal for an August evening."

"Excellent!" exclaimed Melissa, checking her wristwatch. "So we'll see what changes occur when we monitor these same areas at midnight, then again at three and five o'clock in the morning. We need to log normal nights in the valley, so we'll be able to compare any changes that might indicate psychic phenomenon on the actual anniversary."

Daniel looked horrified. "Well, don't wake me up!"

Beth linked her arm tightly through her dad's. "Does that mean I'll be on my own in the middle of the night?"

"Only for short periods," Len reassured her. "And we won't be far away. Tell you what, I'll leave you my mobile. It's got Andrew's and Melissa's numbers in. Just call us if you're at all worried."

Daniel glanced at his mobile phone. "Well I can't get a signal on mine."

Melissa raised one eyebrow. "And remember, of course, any calls to your fathers will show up on our monitors. So please do only ring if it's a real emergency...that's if you can get a signal."

"Well mine's useless!" Daniel shrugged, putting his phone back into his pocket. Then he noticed Beth's long face and gave her a friendly nudge. "You can have the guard dog in your tent, if you want."

Her face lit up. "Scooby? Oh! Can I?"

"Yeah! She'll guard you from any marauding bunny wabbits."

"Oh, wow! Brilliant...thanks!" And she scooped Scooby up into her arms and danced around. "You're going to sleep in my tent...that is all right, isn't it, Dad?"

Len gave a little chuckle. "Sure, if it's okay with Daniel."

"I'd better exercise her before bed," said Daniel, retrieving his pet before she got dizzy. "We don't want any little accidents, do we? Come on, matey."

They wandered out into the darkness, away from the tents, away from the lamplight. Scooby plodded on ahead, tail wagging, occasionally turning back to make a leap at Daniel's trainer laces.

The moon looked like a huge silver pendant hanging over the loch, illuminating the water and changing it into a vast shining glass floor. Gazing up as he walked, Daniel could easily make out the man-in-the-moon's face. He knew it was actually craters and mountains on the moon's surface, but on nights like this, it was easy to imagine it was a huge shining face, smiling down on them.

Strolling on, the sounds of conversation faded until they were just soft muffled murmurs somewhere far behind him. The silence of the valley descended suddenly like a thick, heavy blanket. Now all he could hear were his own footsteps crushing the grass and Scooby's snufflings as she zigzagged on ahead.

Quite suddenly, a barricade of trees loomed before him, massive and imposing, like a blockade of huge and defiant shadowy giants.

Daniel halted instantly, suddenly realizing how far he'd strayed from their camp.

"Not that way, Scooby!" His voice shattered the silence and a wave of startled rustlings and squeaks filled the air. Daniel turned back. The forest was black...and creepy. It wasn't a place to go this time of night.

But Scooby had other ideas. She trotted on, tail wagging, heading straight for the trees.

"Scooby, come back!" Daniel yelled. But the pup was almost out of sight – just an insignificant pale blob in the darkness.

"Scooby, heel!" He could feel panic rising, like a tight band across his chest, and his voice sounded shaky. He made a dash towards his pet but Scooby shot mischievously away. "No! No, Scooby! Come back! Here, girl...here..."

The pale puppy outline grew dimmer and a second later it had gone – swallowed up by a dark and unfriendly forest.

Heart thudding wildly, Daniel bolted after her, desperate to catch Scooby before she scampered too deep into the woods and got totally lost.

With only the moonlight to light his way, he stumbled on, unable to see where he was putting his feet, running blindly, expecting to trip at any second. Then blackness swamped him as the imposing army of trees closed in around him.

There was no sign of Scooby.

chapter three

"**S**cooby!" Daniel yelled, feeling sick with panic. He stood, breathing heavily, surrounded by towering monsters, and for a second he was positive he heard a great sigh. As if the forest was eager for company, whether as welcome visitors...or hapless prey.

Or maybe his mind was playing tricks on him and it was just the sound of the breeze through the branches. He stood, heart pounding, desperate to hear the familiar barking of his pet. But only the cold void of silence greeted him.

A battalion of trees circled him. Some stood upright like soldiers. Others were bent and twisted, like grisly old men, trying to peer around to see who was there. Moonlight glinted through the branches, casting shadows and streaks of light.

"Scooby!" he called, his voice trembling. "Scooby, please..."

A sudden rustling made him jump, and then Scooby came skittering out of the shadows, straight at Daniel, colliding with his legs and whining to be picked up.

Daniel was so relieved that tears stung his eyes. He quickly scooped up his pet and clutched her tightly, his lips pressed against the puppy's head. "You bad dog, you had me worried." The little dog was trembling – and she wasn't the only one.

Holding her tightly, Daniel made his way out of the forest, his eyes darting left and right, barely daring to imagine what had made Scooby skitter back like that.

The pale grey loch stretched out before him – along with a great black expanse of dark valley.

He walked swiftly, continually glancing back, afraid that something was nearby, watching them... stalking them... He suddenly wished he'd never read that newspaper cutting. Now the words jumped into his head.

It stalked us... My brother and I had to run for our lives.

He was sweating. His T-shirt was sticking to his skin and his heart was pounding so crazily it was like a drum in his ears.

The moon hovering low over the loch no longer beamed a friendly smile. Now it had an eerie, unnatural glow, almost as if it were leering at him.

In the distance, Endrith Mountain looked like a painting on a backdrop. Midway across the valley, a cluster of orange lamps flickered like beacons through the blackness. Daniel made a beeline towards them.

He walked briskly, clutching Scooby tightly, until he could hear the murmur of voices and make out figures illuminated in the tents' lamplight.

Beth was standing in the open awning of the big tent, peering out into the blackness. Daniel waved, but knew she couldn't see him. It occurred to him how conspicuous the camp was, stuck in the middle of wild open countryside. How easily they could be picked off in the night if any dangerous predators were on the prowl.

"Foxes and badgers, that's all you get round here, Scooby," he told his pet, speaking unnaturally loudly, trying to quell the thumping of his heart. "Maybe deer, but nothing nasty, like bears or wolves or—" He stopped himself. He wasn't going to start thinking stupid thoughts about ghostly tigers. Instead he shouted to Beth, "Hey! We're over here!"

He wanted to run, only Beth might think he was scared of the dark, so he lengthened his stride, and called out chattily, "Bit dark out here! Have you seen that moon? Great, isn't it!"

She spotted him and ran out to meet him. "There you are! I was getting worried."

"We're okay, we had a nice walk, didn't we, Scooby?" he lied.

Beth fell into step beside him, running to keep up. He hadn't realized how fast he'd been walking. Now he deliberately slowed down.

"Sure you don't mind Scooby sleeping in my tent?" Beth asked, still jogging alongside.

"No problem," he replied, determined not to glance back to see if anything was following.

Beth cast him a puzzled look. "Are you okay, Daniel?"

"Yeah! Why wouldn't I be?"

"You look a bit scared."

"Scared!" exclaimed Daniel. "What's there to be scared about? It's this weird moonlight." He shrugged, glad to finally step into the lamplight where the adults were all still huddled over their ghostbusting equipment. Taking a deep, steadying breath, he asked cheerily, "Spotted any ghosts yet?"

"Not yet," Melissa answered. She glanced up briefly, then did a double take and peered curiously at him over the rim of her spectacles. "*You* haven't seen one, have you?"

"Me?" Daniel laughed. "That'll be the day!"

* * *

Daniel felt hot breath on his face. Two slitted, menacing yellow eyes bore down on him. Frozen with terror, he was desperate to run, to scream, but he couldn't move. He was paralysed by the weight pressing down on him, holding him captive, pinning his arms to his sides. Now black lips curled back to reveal two long sharp sabre teeth, and drops of saliva dripped onto his face.

With a gasp, Daniel sat bolt upright in his sleeping bag, sending a surprised puppy skittering across the tent floor.

With a *woof!* Scooby bounded back to stand on Daniel's chest again, tail wagging madly, a warm little tongue giving him a wash.

"Scooby! You gave me such a fright! How did you get in here? I thought you were a... Oh, never mind!" And he fussed Scooby madly to say sorry for sending her flying.

Voices were drifting in from outside, along with a delicious aroma of sizzling bacon. The fresh morning air soon blew away the last fading remnants of his nightmare.

"Good morning!" everyone greeted him.

He yawned. "I thought you lot were going ghost hunting through the night?"

"We did," said his dad, handing him a mug of tea. "You were sound asleep."

"I heard you coming and going," said Beth, a plate of bacon and eggs balanced on her lap. "Luckily, I had a big brave guard dog cuddled up beside me, so I was fine!"

Melissa was leafing through a little folklore book. "I say, everyone, here's a chapter about the Battle of Endrith – it's rather interesting." She glanced up from the book. "Gentlemen, as the anniversary is the day after tomorrow, we need to be extra vigilant with our data recording so we can make accurate comparisons when checking for psychic phenomena."

"So what's happening today then?" Daniel asked, tucking into his breakfast.

"A spot of fishing, I think," said Daniel's dad, glancing hopefully towards the loch.

But Melissa had other ideas. "Actually I thought we might take readings for paranormal activity around the mountain area. That Laird child thought she first glimpsed the beast zigzagging its way down the mountainside. It was in daylight, too, so that optimizes our time here."

Daniel quietly groaned. Great! Ghost hunting by day and by night!

They set off to investigate Endrith Mountain like an expedition team about to scale Mount Everest. The adults went equipped with hiking boots and haversacks packed with masses of ghostbusting stuff. Daniel and Beth took drinks and a ball.

The majesty of the mountain created a growing sense of awe for Daniel as they got closer. It was just so fantastically enormous.

Beneath their feet the flower-speckled earth became rocky as it rose in a gentle slope. Soon, they were climbing steeper ground and clambering over rocks and boulders that had crumbled from the mountain over the ages and now lay embedded in the earth, gathering moss.

Eventually, the adults stopped to take readings.

Beth looked anxious. "What's supposed to

have happened here, Dad?" she asked.

"That Laird girl reckons she saw something zigzagging down the mountain like a streak of light," Len explained, checking the small ion monitor in his hand, then gazing up at the mountain. "And as you know, light travels in a straight line. It doesn't usually zigzag."

"So you think it was the beast?" Beth suggested, looking serious.

"It makes sense," interrupted Melissa, hoisting herself up onto a flat slab of rock, where she stood as tall as her short, plump frame would allow.

She turned her face to the sky, her hair blowing wildly in the breeze. Then, raising her arms upwards, she called out, "Creature of the past, show yourself to us. We mean you no harm!"

Daniel and Beth stared at each other. Daniel grinned.

"I sense you are near!" Melissa called out again. "Let us feel your presence, oh mighty beast!"

"She's nuts!" Daniel hissed at Beth, trying his best not to laugh. But Beth clearly didn't find it funny, and edged closer to her dad.

"We wish only to make contact with you!" Melissa continued. "Give us a sign. Give us some indication of your presence..."

Everyone stood motionless. Even Scooby stood perfectly still as they all stared at the madwoman on the rock, trying to summon up a ghost.

Daniel was itching to crack a joke, but his dad cast him a stern glance warning him not to even think about it.

Melissa chanted on. "Oh beast! Spirit of lost worlds, show yourself to us. Give us a sign. Prove to us that you exist..." She glanced down at Andrew and hissed, "Get the camcorder ready."

Beth was practically cowering behind her dad now, while Len studied his ion detector intently. Andrew obeyed orders and focused the camcorder on the mountainside.

Melissa remained standing on the rock, arms raised high, her hair and clothing billowing in the breeze, a faraway look glazing her face. Softly she murmured, "I *know* the beast is close by. I *feel* its presence," and she pressed her fingertips to her temples, her eyelids fluttering wildly.

Daniel imitated her, hoping to make Beth giggle and stop looking so worried. Couldn't she see that Melissa was totally batty? She'd got more chance of getting blood out of a stone than summoning up a prehistoric ghost.

Scooby suddenly started to bark.

"Keep the dog quiet!" Melissa hissed, her fingers still pressed to her skull and her eyes tightly shut. "And if you're going to mock, Daniel Glenn, do it elsewhere."

His dad shot him another warning glance and Daniel shrugged innocently, although he couldn't help wondering how Melissa knew what he was doing with her eyes shut.

"The spirit world is very susceptible to atmosphere and attitude," she said in a softly monotonous voice, almost as if she was reading his mind. "If a spirit entity senses that we are mocking or unfriendly, it's hardly likely to cooperate."

She fell silent again and they all stood, silently waiting and watching until Daniel's neck ached from staring up at the mountain for so long, and coloured lights began dancing like rainbow-patterned spots before his eyes. This was getting really boring.

He signalled to Beth to follow him, and whispered to his dad that they were going exploring.

"Not too far now," his dad whispered back, his eye glued to the camcorder viewfinder.

Daniel led the way with Scooby hot on his heels and Beth following. *Let them get on with their stupid ghost hunt*, he thought. *We've got better things to do.*

"Maybe that Laird girl did start seeing things," Daniel remarked, as he picked a route between the moss-strewn boulders. "It makes your eyes go funny, staring at the rock face like that."

"I know," Beth agreed. "But how weird was that? She really scared me! I thought the ghost might really appear – then what would she do?"

For a split second an image flashed through Daniel's head – an image of slitted yellow eyes, snarling black lips and long sabre teeth. He banished the thought and forced himself to laugh.

"Yeah, what? Pat it on the head and say, nice to meet you, Mister Beastie, now would you pose for a picture, and then go back to where you came from, and not eat us up!"

"It's dangerous, isn't it?" Beth said solemnly. "Messing about with spirits and things...I mean, if they *were* real."

"But they're not!" he reminded her. "Now let's forget the madwoman and go cave exploring...see what I see?"

Looking straight ahead they could see a gaping black hole sliced out of the mountainside, like something out of the Flintstones.

"I'm not going in there!" Beth declared, stopping abruptly. "And I don't think you should either."

"Why? It looks wicked!"

"It looks horrible and evil!" she argued, stooping down and hugging Scooby so she didn't wander any nearer to it.

Daniel shrugged. "Stay here then – if you're chicken."

"I'm not chicken, but I'm not stupid either – that looks dangerous!"

Ignoring her, Daniel scrambled over the rocks to reach the shadowy entrance, and then hesitated. An unpleasant chill was oozing from the black hole, as if the sun had never touched it. But he couldn't turn back now. Warily he ventured in, gazing all around as his eyes grew accustomed to the gloom.

"Hello!" he called out, and heard his voice echo back from the deep chasm. "It goes back a long way... Hey, Beth, listen to this echo!"

"Just be careful! Don't go too far!" she called back.

He stepped forward cautiously. Now he could see clammy damp walls and what looked like scratches in the rock. The floor was solid stone, covered in thick dust, and above, jagged protrusions hung down – stalactites or stalagmites? He could never remember which was which.

"It looks spooky!" Beth said suddenly.

Daniel turned to find Beth standing at the cave entrance, silhouetted against the daylight, Scooby clutched in her arms.

"Yeah, a bit spooky, I suppose. It's great

though, don't you think? Wish I'd brought a torch. There could be bats in here, and I bet cavemen lived here, tens of thousands of years ago. Or it could have been an animal's den."

"Not the—"

"Don't even go there!" Daniel stopped her before she scared herself silly again.

"But it's big enough. Maybe this was its lair when it was alive," Beth suggested, keeping well back. "We ought to tell the grown-ups. They should check it out with their equipment." Her voice became a whisper. "Maybe its spirit is still here."

"You're forgetting, ghosts don't exist," Daniel reminded her as he explored deeper, swallowed up by the gloom of the cave. "Besides, I can't feel a weird atmosphere, can you? It's cold, but it doesn't feel *ghostly*, does it?"

"How do we know?" Beth shrugged. "You need all that ghost-hunting stuff to check. Or you have to be weird like Melissa... Haven't you seen enough yet, Daniel? Scooby and I are getting cold."

"I suppose...can't see much anyway," he said, turning and heading back to Beth and his dog waiting at the cave entrance. Scooby gave a ferocious little "woof!" as he emerged from the gloom. "Hey! It's only me!" Daniel assured her, and his pet instantly wagged her tail excitedly as she saw who it was.

"I'm going back to my dad," Beth said, clambering down over the rocks to go back the way they'd come. But she'd only gone a little way when she stopped abruptly. "Oh no! Look where he is! He'll fall!"

Len was climbing up the rock face, way above everyone's heads, while Melissa stood below, calling out her orders and pointing.

"He's much too high," Beth fretted. "That's dangerous! Doesn't that stupid woman care if he falls?"

"Obviously not," said Daniel, deciding to lead Beth off in another direction. They could tell the adults about the cave later, when they weren't so busy. "She cares about one thing – and that's finding the ghost of the beast. Come on, stop worrying. Your dad's used to heights, he's a scaffolder, remember? He'll be okay."

"I hope so..." she murmured, reluctantly following him.

They picked their way downhill, with Beth constantly glancing back until the adults were out of sight. Then they followed a little stream as it cascaded over pebbles and stones. Scooby scampered along the grassy banks, paddling in the shallows, lapping at its crystal cold water and barking at twigs that floated by.

"I like Scotland, don't you?" Daniel remarked as they ambled along. "It's nice – the scenery and everything."

"It's beautiful!" Beth sighed. "I just wish we were on a normal holiday, without all this ghostly stuff. It's horrible thinking about stupid ghosts all the time."

"Yes, but we wouldn't be here if not for the ghosts," Daniel reminded her. "Anyway, it keeps the grown-ups happy."

"*Happy?*" Beth wailed. "That Melissa won't be happy till she's persuaded a sabre-toothed tiger to call in for tea! Honestly, the way she was trying to tune in to the beast's wavelength, like she was mentally trying to contact it..."

"She's potty, ignore her. Besides, if that ghost was real, loads of people would have reported seeing it, and they haven't...just a couple of kids."

Beth didn't look convinced. "Well, so long as Melissa doesn't do anything really stupid or dangerous."

"Ah, forget her. Hey, watch this." He took a ball from his pocket and threw it for Scooby. "Fetch, girl!"

With a woof, the puppy scampered after it, and then stood barking at it.

"She's forgotten what to do," Beth said, managing a little smile. "Come on, Scooby, I'll show you."

Beth fetched the ball herself, and waggled it in front of Scooby's nose. "See, it's a ball, I throw it – you fetch it back."

Eventually Scooby got the hang of the game, but not until after a whole lot of yapping and laughter.

For such a little dog, she had a loud, high-pitched bark. It was a sound that carried easily across the peaceful Valley of Shadows.

*   *   *

High upon a jagged mountain ledge that was bare but for a few tiny pink flowers that scratched life amongst the barren rocks, a presence stirred.

A large presence. Invisible to the human eye, or even to the sharp eye of a hawk.

But here on this stark rocky ledge, an invisible tail flicked, invisible eyelids fluttered, invisible claws unfurled.

Yap, yap, yap...yap, yap, yap...

Like an annoying mosquito buzzing around Karbel's head, the noise prodded at his subconscious mind, wakening him from a deep, deep sleep.

Karbel opened his yellow eyes slowly. For a second as he registered the sound of the puppy barking, memories flooded through his mind. Memories of his siblings, of companionship and play, and a mother's love.

For a fleeting instant, just before he awoke, he was back with his family as a young cub...

And then the memory he thought he had banished from his soul returned – his family wiped out, leaving him orphaned, to grow up alone. The memory was from so far back in time, yet it could almost have been yesterday. And he howled out in anguish as the reality of his solitude returned.

Alone in life – alone in death.

But his cry was silent. No ferocious tiger's roar echoed over the valley to instil terror into those who heard it.

No one could hear the silent roar of a beast that had been dead for thousands of years. Its only effect was to unsettle a hawk on a nearby ledge. Sensing an unseen danger, the bird launched itself swiftly into the air and took flight.

Karbel rose slowly to his feet. He stretched out his massive, lithe spirit form and gazed out across the valley to see what had awoken him – and worse, what had nudged so painfully at memories of when he was alive.

Karbel's eyes were no longer restricted by mortal sight and his gaze swiftly settled on the young humans and the cub.

A wave of memories swept through his mind, stabbing painfully at his heart. Memories of softness and warmth. Of tussles and play fights with his brothers and sisters, rolling in long fresh grass and catching dragonflies. Stalking small creatures, chasing and pouncing on them, pawing and playing with them, until they ceased trying to escape. And finally, discovering how good they tasted.

With a heavy ache in his breast Karbel fixed his sharp yellow eyes on the small cub, scampering and yapping besides a stream. In spirit form Karbel had no physical hunger or thirst to satisfy, but his memories recalled how good warm flesh tasted. It could almost be yesterday that he had stalked, killed and devoured a small animal such as this.

The cub was small and fat. Its movements were slow and ungainly.

It would be an easy kill.

Making no sound, disturbing not a fleck of dust, he sprang from his ledge, leaping down the mountainside, zigzagging his way from ridge to ridge, boulder to boulder.

Near the base, he stopped sharply, encountering more humans – a female and two males. They were holding weapons – strange weapons. And humans with weapons meant death.

Defiantly he roared into the female human's face and lashed out with a massive, taloned paw. Razor sharp claws sliced through her mercilessly.

But his spirit made no impact. They were so close, yet on such different planes, that their worlds could never touch.

Yet, the female collapsed to the ground.

Karbel leaped over her crumpled body as the males ran to her aid. Humans were dangerous creatures. It had been a human who had taken his life. They were to be avoided. They had the power over life and death.

But small fat cubs were food – and suddenly Karbel felt hungry.

chapter four

"Melissa! Are you all right? Can you hear me? Are you hurt?"

Andrew and Len huddled over Melissa as she lay motionless, her eyes wide open, staring, her skin ashen. "Melissa!" Andrew felt for a pulse in her throat. "Speak to me, Melissa, have you hit your head?"

Suddenly she snatched at Andrew's hand,

alert, eyes like saucers. "The beast!" she breathed. "It's here! I felt its presence! Check the monitors, quickly, check them. Something must have registered..."

Andrew patted her hand instead. "All in good time, just lie still for a minute. I think you tripped and banged your head. You're a bit concussed, I'd say. Just take it easy."

"I am not concussed!" Melissa snapped, struggling to get up. "And I didn't bang my head! I'm telling you the beast was here...*right here*! It was the most powerful surge of energy I have ever felt in my life."

Pushing the men aside, she scrambled to her feet and picked up her electromagnetic field meter. She held it out, elated. "Look at this! It's gone completely off the scale. It's registered extraordinary levels and jammed."

"Hang on, Melissa, I think most likely you damaged it when you fell," suggested Len, trying to steady her. "Readings of this nature are simply unparalleled. There's never been anything of this magnitude."

She shrugged his hand away and snatched Andrew's meter, which digitally recorded variations in temperature. "How about this then? Or did this monitor miraculously break at the same time? Look at these readings!" Her voice became shrill. "Well, what's your explanation for this?"

The two men exchanged glances as they double-checked the monitors. Andrew rubbed his chin. "Well, it certainly indicates a major disturbance."

"Exactly!" she practically screamed. "Minus two degrees, shooting up to forty-one degrees, then back to normal fifteen degrees – all within a minute!"

Len took a closer look and raised one eyebrow. "Well, I've got to admit, that's pretty odd."

"It was the beast," she breathed, her eyes shining. "Gentlemen, there is no doubt about it. We are in the presence of the ghost of a prehistoric sabre-toothed tiger."

Karbel stood on a flat grey rock and raised his huge fanged head to the breeze. Instantly he picked up on the scent of the cub, and a trickle of saliva dripped from his jaws. It fell onto the rock where it remained like a shining gem as the beast turned into the breeze and padded swiftly and purposefully towards the unsuspecting puppy.

Scooby had now brought the ball back a record ten times without getting it wrong, although she clearly thought it necessary to bark excitedly in between every throw.

"I think she's got the hang of it," Daniel remarked, tripping over something that was lying in the long grass. "Hey, look at this," he said, picking up a curved stick. "It's a bit like a Highlander's sword, don't you think?"

Beth cast him a sympathetic smile. "No, it looks like a broken bit of wood. Come on, Daniel, I need to check on my dad – I need to make sure he hasn't fallen off that mountain."

"He'll be fine." Daniel dismissed her worries, swirling the stick like a swordsman. "On guard!"

"Careful! You'll have my eye out!"

Scooby dropped the ball at his feet and barked expectantly. "Throw it for her, would you, Beth? I have a battle to fight."

"How old are you?" She laughed, avoiding the swirling bit of wood as she threw the ball.

Scooby went scampering off again, ears flapping, tail wagging madly. Then she stopped, abruptly, skidding to a halt with a startled yelp. The next second, she turned tail and came skittering back, tail between her legs, ears pressed to the sides of her head, puppy eyes wide with terror.

She practically clawed her way up Daniel's legs and into his arms, desperately trying to hide under his armpit, all the time whimpering pitifully.

"Hey! What's up, matey?" Daniel asked, bemused. "Scared of your own shadow? Fear not, for I, Daniel MacGlenn, will defend you..." And with his best imitation of a swordsman, he advanced, swirling, jabbing and lunging at thin air with his stick.

Beth stood there laughing. "Daniel, you are an idiot!"

"Well Scooby doesn't think so. See, she's

stopped trembling now. Go on, down you go, girl." He set Scooby on the ground. "She probably saw a bee or maybe even a snake. They have snakes around here, y'know."

The moment Scooby was on the ground, she instantly pranced forward a few steps, then stood defiantly, her hackles raised and gave the deepest, most ferocious little *woof*!

It was such a brave little woof, that both Daniel and Beth burst out laughing.

Melissa was hyper. She was gabbling so madly that Daniel and Beth hadn't a clue what she was talking about when they wandered back to the adults again.

"What's up with her?" Daniel asked his dad.

Andrew rubbed his chin. "Well, we seem to have hit upon something pretty odd. A couple of the monitors have registered enormous surges, both in electromagnetic fields and temperature fluctuations, and..." He glanced at Beth and instantly fell silent.

"And what?" she demanded, looking at everyone in turn. "And what? Dad?"

Len put his arm around her. "Melissa thinks she felt some kind of inexplicable *presence*, that's all..."

"Not an *inexplicable* presence at all," Melissa contradicted, her eyes sparkling wildly. "It was the beast! It's here. I felt its presence, it was huge, immense. It's so powerful, I could *feel* it..."

"Dad!" Beth cried, clutching his arm. "I don't like it, it's freaky...I'm scared."

For a second, Len glared at Melissa as if he'd like to throttle her, but she was too busy rooting about in her rucksack to worry herself about upsetting anyone. Taking a deep breath, Len calmly spoke to Beth. "Beth, love – there's nothing to be scared about. There's nothing to harm us, I promise. Now stop looking so worried."

Melissa had taken out a notepad and pencil. She settled herself on a flat rock and began writing, her hand skimming across the notepad as if she couldn't get it all down fast enough. "Ignore me," she called out with a dismissive wave. "I've a report to write."

Shaking his head, Daniel wandered a little way off with his dad, leaving mad Melissa scribbling away and Len still trying to convince Beth that there was nothing freaky about this trip at all. "So what exactly happened, Dad?" Daniel asked, keeping his voice low so Beth wouldn't hear.

"Well, son, it was really weird," Andrew exclaimed. He was trying to retain his usual dignified *police officer* manner, but Daniel saw the excited gleam in his eye and guessed that whatever had happened, it was definitely something out of the ordinary. "Everything was normal one minute then the next second Melissa was spark out on the ground. At first I thought she'd slipped or fainted. But she was adamant that she'd felt a massive surge of energy which completely floored her. And actually the surge did register dramatically on our monitors. In fact I've never seen readings like this before. There certainly was something very unusual going on for a moment or two."

"Well, it's certainly got *her* excited," Daniel remarked, jerking his head in Melissa's direction. "I bet when she sees the cave Beth and I discovered, she'll go all weird about that as well."

"What cave is this then, Daniel?"

He shrugged. "Just a cave, we thought it might have been an animal's lair at some time..."

His dad looked steadily at him. "An animal's lair. Do you mean...?"

"Hey, you're the ghostbuster, not me."

"Well, you'd better show us where it is...see if that's going to reveal any secrets." His dad cast him an eager smile. "I'll go and amass the troops!"

They all set off, with Daniel striding ahead, swinging his wooden Highland sword which had now become a walking stick, and Scooby scampering excitedly at his heels.

Melissa marched beside him, while the others tagged along behind – with Beth hanging onto her dad's arm for all she was worth.

It was easy enough to retrace their steps, and after a few minutes of negotiating some massive slabs of moss-covered granite, the sinister black cave loomed up ahead. "There it is!" Daniel announced.

Melissa stopped and gazed up at it, her face stunned in awe for a second. "Yes!" she breathed, as if she knew it was the beast's lair for certain. And then she leaped into action, scrambling over the rocks to reach the eerie shadowy entrance. "Hurry up, chaps, we need to get those monitors set up," she called back.

Everyone followed her, except Beth, who picked up Scooby and hung well back, clutching the puppy safely in her arms.

"Pretty spooky, don't you think?" Daniel grinned, climbing faster than the grown-ups and then casually sauntering into the cave mouth.

"Wow!" exclaimed Len, catching him up and flashing the beam from his torch around the inside of the cavern. "This is pretty awesome. Just look at those stalactites!"

Daniel ventured deeper as streaks of torchlight criss-crossing around the cave walls illuminated the way. Behind him, the adults checked their monitors as they went.

"It's cold in here, but that's probably normal," remarked Andrew, his voice echoing around the dark chasm. "Are you picking up on anything, Len?"

"Not sure, mate, there's a slight electromagnetic disturbance registering, nothing you can really put your finger on though... Melissa, what do you think?"

After her rush to reach the cave, Melissa now seemed reluctant to go any further. Her step was slow, wary, almost like someone testing the water with their toes. Her eyes looked luminous behind her spectacles and the light from the detecting device in her hand shone up into her face, giving her an eerie glow. Her voice was little more than a whisper. "Nothing as yet, all very normal."

The cavern narrowed as Daniel wandered further into its gloom. With his dad and Len close by, he was more confident about exploring deeper.

His dad's torchlight illuminated some scratches on the wall. Daniel ran his hand over them, shuddering at the damp, slimy feel of ancient rock.

"Look at these, Dad – cave drawings."

"Might only be graffiti, son," his dad's voice echoed back. "You'd need to be an archaeologist to know if they are genuine."

Despite the slime, Daniel traced his fingers

over the figures etched into the rock. One was like a stick drawing of a man, and there was another, of an animal – a large animal if you compared it with the stick man, with big, long teeth...or rather, fangs.

"Dad, look at this—"

"Temperature's fallen!" Len suddenly interrupted. "Big drop! And I mean *big*!"

"Magnetic fluctuations recording," Andrew stated, striding across to where Len was standing.

"There's an orb!" came Melissa's excited hiss. "I can definitely see an orb! See...at the very back of the cave – that small spot of light, that's an orb."

"Zero degrees!" Len warned. "Still going down, minus one..." Daniel felt it too, an icy coldness, chilling his bones, sending shivers down his spine. Suddenly monitors began beeping, red lights flashing. No one was interested in his cave drawings any more.

Beth appeared in the mouth of the cave, clutching the pup. "Dad!" she called. "Hurry up! I don't like being out here on my own."

Chaos erupted.

Melissa suddenly let out an ear-piercing scream, spun like a ballerina, and fell to her knees. At the same second, Scooby started yelping and wriggling crazily in Beth's arms. Beth cried out, struggling to hold on to the puppy.

Daniel ran to help her as the two dads dashed towards Melissa, who was slumped on the cave floor.

Scooby was desperate to be free. "Scooby! It's okay, calm down, girl... Let me have her, Beth," Daniel said, taking her before she could escape. "It's okay, girl, it's okay." He glared at Melissa, who was on the floor, shaking. He guessed that her scream had startled Scooby into a panic, although what she'd found to scream at was anyone's guess. The woman was a complete maniac. His dad was still bent over Melissa, but Len came dashing over to Beth and steered her out into the sunlight.

Daniel spoke soothingly to his pet, stroking her softly. Finally, Scooby calmed down and stopped trying to get away. Holding the trembling pup in his arms, he went over to where Beth and her dad were huddled together. "What was all that about..." His mouth dropped open when he saw Beth's face. It was covered in blood. A dark red trickle was oozing from a gash in her forehead and dribbling down her face.

Len pressed a handkerchief to the wound. "Okay, no panic. It's not as bad as it looks. Scratches to the forehead always bleed heavily."

Daniel felt sick. "Did Scooby do that? She didn't mean to, she was just struggling... Scooby, say you're sorry. You're a bad dog!"

"I'm all right, it wasn't her fault," Beth said shakily, doing her best not to cry as her dad pressed the cloth firmly over the scratch. "She was scared – when Melissa screamed, she just panicked."

Melissa emerged shakily from the cave, with Andrew holding her up. Her face was as white as chalk.

Daniel was suddenly furious with the stupid woman. "What freaked you out?" he yelled angrily. "You panicked Scooby and made her scratch Beth's face. Look at her, she's bleeding!"

Melissa took a few more unsteady steps and vaguely raised her right hand to point over their heads – towards the valley and the forest. And then she spoke. Her voice was hushed, but everyone heard the words she uttered before she collapsed again.

"The beast!"

chapter five

Somehow they all staggered back to camp.
Scooby refused to be set down and whined every
time Daniel tried. Beth had a piggyback from her
dad, and Melissa reluctantly linked her arm
through Andrew's as he supported her across the
wide expanse of valley.

Back at camp, Scooby whimpered and
scratched at Daniel's tent to be allowed in, and the

moment he unzipped it, the pup dived down to the bottom of his sleeping bag, and stayed there.

Leaving her, Daniel wandered back to the walking wounded. Melissa had collapsed into a camping chair, and Len was cleaning up Beth's scratch while his dad got busy making tea.

Melissa raised her pale eyes and looked directly at Daniel. "Your dog senses the beast's presence," she murmured. "Just as I did... Dogs can be sensitive to the supernatural at times."

Daniel didn't answer her. Instead he wandered over to Beth and Len. "Are you okay?"

She gave a little nod, but Daniel thought she looked far from okay. Feeling quite miserable, he decided to go and keep Scooby company.

He peered into the sleeping bag and Scooby peeped out with big doleful eyes.

"What happened to you, matey?" Daniel asked, reaching in to gently stroke Scooby's soft silky face. "Did the silly woman scare you, screaming like that? You know she's nuts. Now she's making out you're as weird as her. Sensitive to the supernatural? As if! You're just sensitive to maniac women screaming and scaring the life out of you, aren't you!" He reached in and lifted his pet into his arms. "And I know you didn't mean to scratch Beth, she's forgiven you, so don't worry."

Scooby's little tail wagged sheepishly and she tentatively licked Daniel's nose.

"That's better. Come on! Let's go get you a nice doggy chew."

Giving her a final cuddle, Daniel found a chew and went out into the August sunlight with Scooby scampering after him, eager now to have her doggy treat. Daniel made her sit before giving it to her.

"Good girl!"

Holding it in her mouth, the pup trotted proudly off and flopped down at the side of Melissa's tent to enjoy it.

Melissa was holding court – sitting there with her monitors, reliving her latest psychic experience, while everyone else listened intently as they drank their tea.

"It was just like before, only even more intense," she was saying, her eyes looking wilder than usual. "Just as you reported those temperature changes I felt this incredible blast of energy sweep right through me. It just spun me around and I felt this tremendous icy coldness followed by an intense heat..."

Daniel picked up the mug of tea that was waiting for him and reluctantly sat down with them all, although he couldn't help thinking that he was a bit too old for fairy stories.

As Melissa went on with her story, Daniel closed his eyes against the summer sunlight. Its brightness was causing the loch to glint with light and movement. It was a strange kind of daylight. If anyone had been looking, they might have noticed that it seemed to have created a heat haze near the shores of the lake.

A shimmering heat haze.

A shimmering, flickering mass of light – drifting one way and then the other.

Back and forth...back and forth.

Like something pacing...

If anyone had spotted the odd apparition, they would undoubtedly have put it down to a trick of the light or a reflection off the water. But the light mass seemed to be taking on a form. It no longer drifted, but moved with stealth and power, yet it passed over the long grass without so much as bending a blade or crushing a flower petal.

A wavering mass of energy that moved with purpose and determination...and a growing sense of fury.

That cub would be his! Karbel could almost taste its torn flesh.

But he needed to grow strong, to amass all his energies to become mortal just long enough to snatch and devour his prey.

Twice, he had been close enough. The first time the young male had charged at him with a weapon, lunging and jabbing at him until he withdrew.

And then, just a short while ago, he had tried to drag the cub from the young female's grasp, but his attempt was frustrated. He wasn't yet powerful enough to overcome even a puny human, although he had drawn blood. He had smelled it. If he had been in full manifestation, his attack would have sliced her into shreds.

He snarled, growing impatient. His belly was rumbling – he must have food.

Scooby lay splayed on her tummy, gripping the doggy treat in her front paws, contentedly chewing. She paused for a moment to nibble a blade of sweet-smelling grass. And then she investigated a bug crawling over a clump of white clover.

Lying in the long grass, Scooby couldn't see the loch, couldn't see the shimmering mass of light that paced back and forth. And didn't notice when the hazy apparition suddenly changed direction.

No longer did it move back and forth. It turned and headed directly towards the camp – and the small unsuspecting puppy lazing in the August sunshine.

Scooby chewed on, oblivious, as the strange presence flattened itself to the ground, moving slower, more stealthily...

If Scooby had glanced up – if the chew hadn't tasted so good, if the bug hadn't been quite so fascinating – she might have seen the monstrous apparition creeping up on her.

But the chew *was* good, and it needed her total concentration...

The shimmering mass of unearthly light glided closer. Stopping and starting, flattened to the earth, slinking nearer with every second...

Suddenly it was there! An immense power that shrouded the little puppy. A terrifying form that had no smell, no substance, but oozed danger – and death.

A squeak of terror was the only sound Scooby made as she instinctively rolled onto her back in submission, her belly and throat bared to this deadly invisible predator.

At the sound of his pet's whimper, Daniel opened his eyes and saw Scooby on her back – lying so still...

He shot out of his chair. "Scooby!"

In three strides he was there, snatching Scooby up, terrified in case she'd choked on her chew.

That very same second a flash of light exploded in front of Daniel's eyes, dazzling him, knocking him off balance. A fleeting sensation of icy coldness engulfed him and then a great blast of heat, as if someone had opened a huge oven door. And a noise, a noise such as he'd never heard before, almost like...he couldn't think. A distant, faraway noise, yet it was here – right here!

Daniel stood reeling, clutching Scooby as his dad rushed over.

"Is she all right? Here, give her to me," Andrew demanded. "Is she choking?" He snatched the puppy and quickly checked its breathing.

Daniel stood trembling, dumbstruck by the weird sensations he'd just experienced.

His dad checked the puppy all over. "It's okay, son, she's breathing. Can't see anything stuck in her throat." He glanced at Daniel then. "She's fine... What was all that about?"

Daniel took his pet back and cuddled her closely, his own heart hammering as rapidly as Scooby's. "I...I don't know. I thought she'd choked. She was lying so still on her back...

I thought she was dead. Then when I picked her up I went really cold, then really hot, and a white light flashed in front of my eyes... It was so weird."

Beth came rushing over, followed by her dad. "What happened? Is Scooby okay?"

"Everyone's fine," Andrew assured her, sidestepping towards her dad. Quietly he murmured, "The lad felt temperature changes, cold then hot and a flash of white light. I can't help thinking..."

Len's eyes darted towards Beth then back at Andrew. "We'll have a chat in a minute, mate, okay?"

Melissa came striding over, ghostbusting monitors in her hands and beaming from ear to ear. Daniel glared at her. What on earth was she looking so pleased about? Didn't she care that Scooby had just choked...or rather, that he thought she had.

"It's perfectly obvious what the boy has just experienced, take a look at these readings!" she exclaimed, holding out the gauges.

"Oh, Dad, not the beast again!" Beth cried, turning her face into her dad's chest.

"No! Of course it's not!" Len instantly dismissed the idea, but Daniel spotted the way they all glanced at each other, and knew that was *exactly* what they were thinking.

A second later his dad gave Daniel's shoulder a friendly squeeze. "Tell you what, son, why don't you kids take Scooby for a little walk? Check her out...if she has swallowed something, she might need to be sick."

For once, Daniel would have preferred to stay and hear what they had to say. It had been a really weird experience. But obviously they didn't want to discuss their freaky, ghosty stuff with Beth listening.

"Okay!" he sighed. "Beth, are you coming? We'll leave the adults to play with their toys." He tried to make a joke of it, but it was hard to be funny when your legs were still shaking.

But Beth didn't want to go anywhere and clung onto her dad. "No way! Not with a horrible sabre-toothed tiger hanging around."

"There's not!" Len practically shouted. "All these weird occurrences are connected to the battle phenomena – it's almost the anniversary. It's a time when certain, sensitive people experience these oddities, but they can't *harm* you." He prised Beth away and held her at arm's length. "Believe me, Beth, there is nothing to be frightened of – nothing!"

"Promise?" Beth murmured, looking a little more reassured.

"Absolutely. You wouldn't be here if there was any danger."

For a few long moments no one spoke, and then Daniel gave Beth a nudge. "Beth, come on, this is getting really boring. Let's go explore the forest."

Reluctantly she followed him, and they headed across the green valley towards the great mass of trees. Despite trying to sound normal, Daniel still felt odd and kept Scooby safely in his arms as they walked.

Maybe Len really thought all this weird stuff was connected to the anniversary of the battle but it seemed to Daniel that he was just trying to stop

Beth getting scared. And it certainly wasn't what Melissa was thinking. She obviously thought he'd had an encounter with the beast.

He glanced back, expecting to see the grownups all huddled around their monitors. He was surprised to see Melissa standing alone – staring after them.

An icy cold shiver ran down his spine.

If she really believed he'd just encountered the beast, maybe she thought it was still hanging around.

Following them...

"Do you think it's the spirits of those warriors, Daniel?" Beth asked softly.

"No!" he stated defiantly, dragging his thoughts back from wondering what Melissa was thinking. "I don't believe in ghosts! I think all these temperature changes are due to some freaky weather phenomenon or something – you hear about them all the time now."

"I hadn't thought of that," Beth said, brightening a little. "Maybe that's what's making their monitors go crazy."

"Yeah, I reckon so," Daniel agreed, trying not to think of those weird sensations he'd felt. They had been real enough.

She cast him a little sympathetic smile. "Daniel, why don't you put Scooby down now? I'm sure she'd love to have a run about."

Daniel hesitated, reluctant to let Scooby go. But then he couldn't hold onto her for ever. Besides, there was absolutely no such thing as ghosts. Melissa was completely dotty, and was just winding everyone up. Making everyone start to think stupid thoughts...

There was nothing here to hurt his dog. There was nothing here to hurt anyone. And to prove it, he placed his pet on the ground. "Go on, Scooby, down you go, girl."

The second Scooby was set down, she charged off – not too far, just a few steps in the direction they'd come, and then stopped. With her hackles raised she barked defiantly – that same funny, brave little *woof* as before.

But this time, it didn't make Daniel laugh.

It made him shiver.

chapter six

The forest in daylight was a nicer place than the forest at night. The statuesque trees and wizened old stumps now seemed to welcome their visitors, as Daniel, Beth and Scooby wandered beneath the leafy canopy. Sunlight through the treetops made everything sparkle. But nothing could shake off the strange foreboding that had settled on Daniel's shoulders.

"I wish you'd stop worrying about Scooby, Daniel," said Beth, ducking beneath a low branch. "She's fine now. Look at her! She's having great fun exploring everything."

"Yeah, I know," Daniel agreed, watching his dog burrowing into piles of leaves and poking her head down rabbit holes. He sighed, wishing he could shift this ominous cloud that was spoiling his day.

It wasn't as if the forest was creepy now, not like it had seemed before. No eerie shadows. The trees looked like trees, not gigantic figures that might uproot and crash down at any second. Rustling sounds were just rabbits scampering through the undergrowth. Fluttering noises overhead were just birds swooping from branch to branch. There was nothing evil or sinister or ghostly about the place. It was just that stupid Melissa twisting everything, turning everything around so it all pointed to the valley being haunted by a sabre-toothed tiger.

"Y'know," murmured Daniel as their feet crunched through the carpet of fallen leaves, "I reckon Melissa just wants her name in the papers, like those Laird kids. I think she's determined to make everything seem sensational, just to get famous."

"You're probably right," Beth agreed, stopping to investigate some fungi growing around a fallen log. It wasn't long before she was engrossed in examining all the odd-looking mushrooms growing from tree trunks, and pointing them out to Daniel every step of the way. "Look at these, aren't they pretty?" she called, finding some red and white spotted toadstools.

"And poisonous! So don't pick them for breakfast," Daniel warned. He was still wondering just how desperate Melissa was to get her name associated with the beast of Endrith Valley.

"I know, I'm not stupid," Beth retorted. "They're actually called fly agarics. But I think they're the sort of toadstools that fairies and elves live in, don't you?"

He groaned. "Don't tell me you believe in fairies now!"

She gasped in horror. "Don't tell me you don't! Every time someone says they don't believe in fairies, one dies... Oh, look..." She bent down and gently scooped up something from the grass. Slowly she walked towards him, gazing sadly into her cupped hands.

"What?" Daniel frowned, suddenly concerned.

"Look what you've done...it's a dead fairy."

"Hey? Don't be daft, it can't be." But he peered anxiously into her hands anyway.

With a shriek of laughter, Beth threw open her empty hands. "Now who believes in fairies?"

"Oh, ha ha!" he groaned, trying not to smile. "Very funny!"

She gave him a friendly nudge. "That's better! You're almost smiling again..."

Her laughter died as a loud crack from behind made them spin around. "What was that?" she breathed.

Scooby heard it too. She looked up, mud on her nose from investigating a rabbit hole.

A shivery sensation crawled up Daniel's back. "I don't know..."

Beth clutched his arm. "It was a twig breaking, a big twig. It was loud. What could have broken a twig that big, Daniel?"

"A deer, maybe. You get deer and stags in this part of the country."

"Will it attack us?" Her voice was shaky, her eyes wide.

"Course not. Actually, we'd be lucky to see a deer," he said positively, aware that his heart was racing. "They camouflage themselves really well in forests. They just merge in with the undergrowth."

"So it was a deer?"

"Probably...maybe..."

"What else could it be?" Her voice still trembled.

Daniel's eyes flitted left and right, all his senses suddenly acutely alert. He could hear insects buzzing, birds fluttering, his heart thudding against his ribcage.

"What's that?" Beth's nails dug into him. "Listen!"

Shushh, shushh... Someone or *something* was disturbing the deep layers of fallen leaves that carpeted the forest.

Scooby gave a little growl.

"Grab Scooby," Beth whispered. "I think we should get out of here."

Shushh, shushh... More footsteps.

Crack! Another twig snapped underfoot.

Daniel reached for his pet, but Scooby shot off, yapping excitedly.

"Scooby!" they both yelled.

And then they saw...it was a man – and Scooby was running straight at him.

"It's my dad!" Daniel gasped, his knees practically buckling with relief. He grinned widely at Beth. "It's just my dad! Hey, Dad, over here."

Beth heaved a massive sigh. "Thank goodness! For a second, I thought it might be Melissa's horrible beast."

Daniel shook his head in despair. "Do me a favour! First it's fairies then it's the beast. You're getting as daft as Melissa!"

Beth gave him another shove. "You're not fooling me, Daniel Glenn. You were as scared as me for a minute."

"Nah! Not me." He grinned, striding off

towards his dad. "Hey, Dad! What are you doing here?"

"Hiya, kids!" Andrew Glenn waved, stooping to fuss Scooby. "You've wandered a bit far, haven't you? I've had a heck of a job finding you."

"Yeah, we're just exploring. Beth's picking mushrooms for breakfast."

"I am not!" she retaliated. "Lots of them are poisonous, I wouldn't risk it."

"Best not," agreed his dad. "So, are you all okay? Just thought I'd catch you up, make sure the pup is all right."

"Yeah, she's great now," said Daniel, and Scooby proved the point by gambolling amongst the leaves.

"And you, Beth? How's your forehead?"

Her fingers touched the plaster on her brow. "A little bit sore, but not too bad, thank you."

They strolled on, enjoying the beauty of the forest as shafts of sunlight made a stripy light-and-shade effect all around.

"So, Beth, what do you think of bonnie Scotland?" asked Andrew.

"Oh! It's beautiful. I think it's the most beautiful place on earth..." Her smile faded. "It's just...well, all this ghosty stuff. I hate all that."

"Don't let it worry you," smiled Andrew. "Nothing's going to harm you."

Daniel's dad was smiling confidently as he spoke, but Daniel spotted the tension in his dad's eyes, and that black heavy cloud settled back on his shoulders.

They spent another hour or so ambling lazily through the forest. It wasn't until they were strolling back across the valley, and Beth ran on ahead to see her dad, that Andrew explained what was on his mind.

"I didn't want to say anything in front of Beth – she's nervy anyway with all this talk of spirits and things."

"Yeah...?" Daniel murmured warily, not sure he wanted to hear what was coming.

"We checked out the monitors Melissa was holding when Scooby had her funny turn and you felt those temperature fluctuations – and there was definitely some strange activity going on."

Daniel's stomach lurched. "Like what?"

His dad looked steadily at him. "Well, like you said, very low and then very high temperatures. Plus, the electromagnetic field monitor went right off the scale." His dad took a deep breath. "Basically, it all points to paranormal activity taking place in that exact location."

"A ghost, you mean?" Daniel could barely say the word. His throat felt parched suddenly and despite the warmth of the day, an icy shiver ran down his spine.

"The readings were identical to those we logged earlier, when Melissa first collapsed, and then in the cave. There were even some EVP readings."

"What are EVPs?"

"Electronic voice phenomena – it sounded like a roar..."

Daniel went icy cold. It *had* sounded like a roar. A roar that was distant – yet right there. Trying hard to stay calm, he said, "So, you reckon it was a ghost then?"

"A spirit entity."

"Yeah...a ghost."

"That's one way of putting it, I suppose."

Daniel stared at his dad. "A ghost that roars! Dad, are you saying it was the ghost of the beast? The ghost of a prehistoric sabre-toothed tiger? The beast that terrorized those Laird kids?"

His dad remained silent.

But the look on his face said it all.

chapter seven

"There you are!" exclaimed Melissa as Daniel and his dad walked silently back into camp. "We were just about to send out a search party! Cold drinks all round, yes? And I've a nice biscuit for the little dog... Here puppy, puppy!" She crouched down, holding out a ginger biscuit to Scooby.

"Actually, I don't like her eating bis—" Too late, Melissa had already fed it to her. "Oh well, one won't hurt I suppose. I just don't want her getting fat."

"Like me, you mean?" Melissa laughed, stroking Scooby as she licked the crumbs from her fingers.

"I didn't mean that." Daniel frowned, wondering why Melissa was being so nice. He guessed she was still hyper now she'd got evidence of her ghost.

She remained annoyingly cheerful for the rest of the afternoon. And as they finished their evening meal, she was practically bubbling with excitement.

"I think I prefer her when she's off with the fairies," said Daniel, as he and Beth played Scrabble under the tent lamplight, with Scooby curled up on Daniel's lap.

"Me too... Oh! Watch out, here she comes."

Melissa poked her head through the tent flap. "We're taking readings near the loch tonight. Coming with us?"

"No thank you," Beth said, politely. "We're playing Scrabble."

"The little dog, then?" she asked brightly. "Bit of exercise before bed and all that."

"No, don't think so, she's pretty exhausted," replied Daniel, holding on to Scooby.

"Oh, that's a shame," Melissa exclaimed, blustering in and reaching out to stroke Scooby.

Daniel cuddled his pet closer – out of reach of those glittering fingers. "She needs her beauty sleep," he said protectively.

Melissa's mouth twitched into a strained kind of smile. "Another time then," she murmured, hesitating before flouncing out again, leaving behind just her flowery, herby scent.

Daniel gritted his teeth and muttered, "I don't think so."

"She's weird," Beth said, zipping the tent flap up after Melissa. "I'm amazed she'd even want Scooby tagging along. I thought she said dogs disturb the paranormal atmosphere... Oh! It's all stupid anyway – trying to make contact with a dead animal! I mean, ghosts of people are bad enough, but you can't communicate with a wild animal when it's *alive*, so how can you when it's been dead for thousands of years?"

"Actually, you've got a good point there,"

agreed Daniel thoughtfully. "You wouldn't call out to a wild animal and expect it to come – that's difficult enough with a pet dog. Shouting to a wild animal would make it run away and hide."

"Exactly!" agreed Beth, placing down her Scrabble letters and adding up her word score. "She is just so idiotic!"

Daniel's thoughts were racing. So just how exactly *did* Melissa expect to summon up the beast, if it existed? She'd tried calling to it, and that didn't work...

Then it came to him. You lured a wild animal with food. And what would sabre-toothed tigers have eaten in prehistoric times? They were carnivores. They ate raw meat!

Words from the newspaper cutting jumped into his head again...

Their sabre teeth would have been used to puncture the soft underbelly of their prey.

Scooby wriggled on his lap and rolled onto her back to have her tummy tickled.

"Daniel, I said it's your turn." Beth broke into his thoughts. "Hello, anyone at home?"

He felt sick. Really, really sick. "What? Sorry, I was miles away." He placed some letters down automatically. Then stared in horror at the word he'd made.

"Oh! Nice one, Daniel," Beth remarked sarcastically. "And it's a triple word score!"

Daniel stared at the Scrabble board. The word he'd spelled was...TIGER.

At breakfast next morning, it was obvious the dads had been talking and had decided to lighten the mood and put ghost-hunting activities on hold for a while.

After the restless night's sleep Daniel had just had, tossing and turning, dreaming about ghosts and sabre-toothed tigers, he was glad to hear they were going to do something different today.

"It's high time we all relaxed and had some fun," said Len, as he cracked eggs into the frying pan.

Andrew emerged from the ghostbusting van,

carrying their blow-up dinghy and paddles. "Hey, kids, fancy going boating after breakfast?"

"You bet!" Daniel yelled, grinning at Beth.

She didn't look quite as convinced, but nodded anyway.

"You'd better wear life jackets," said Len. "And I think we'll moor the boat with a long rope, so we can drag you back if you drop an oar or anything."

"We can take Scooby on board too, can't we?" asked Daniel eagerly.

"I don't see why not," said Andrew, returning to the van for the electric pump. "On strict instructions that you don't mess about. Len and I will be doing a spot of fishing, so we won't be far away."

"And I have notes to write up," announced Melissa, which didn't surprise anyone.

As soon as breakfast was over they inflated the bright yellow dinghy and carried it down to the loch. Scooby ran alongside yapping happily.

Everyone paddled barefoot into the shallows and Len and Andrew held the dinghy steady while

Daniel and Beth lifted Scooby in and then clambered aboard. Len attached the craft to a tree stump with a long rope.

"Hoist the anchor and set sail, me hearties!" Daniel called. Scooby stood in the well of the dinghy on her hind legs, peering eagerly out across the water like an old sea dog.

"No messing about," said Andrew sternly.

"That goes for you too, Beth," warned Len as, with a push, he sent the dinghy drifting off onto the pale grey loch.

It was odd to begin with, feeling the dinghy bobbing and bouncing on the water – it gave a kind of heady feeling. A warm breeze fluttered across the water's surface, creating a pattern of ripples for as far as the eye could see, catching the sun's rays and making everything glint and sparkle.

"This is perfect!" Beth sighed as she relaxed back, trailing her hand in the water.

"Yes, well some of us are doing all the work," Daniel joked, gradually getting the hang of paddling and manoeuvring.

"The loch wouldn't be 250 metres deep this close to shore, would it?"

Daniel poked the paddle downwards, finding that it didn't touch the bottom. "It's deeper than the paddle, so don't fall in."

"I'd be all right. I've got my fifty-metre breaststroke badge. Can't you swim?"

"Yeah! Of course! You'd float anyway with these life jackets on."

Beth sighed happily. "I love the water, don't you? It's just so peaceful and tranquil – and no one's going on about stupid ghosts."

"Very true," Daniel agreed as they drifted and bobbed and enjoyed the magnificent views of forest and mountain that bordered the loch.

"Can I have a go at paddling?" Beth asked after a while.

"If you like," said Daniel, shifting position. The movement caused the dinghy to dip and lurch. "Whoops!"

"Careful! Don't overturn us."

The boat settled again, and Beth took the oars and happily began to paddle across the rippling grey loch. Scooby remained at the helm, loving this new experience and yapping when a drop of water splashed her.

Relaxing back, with his feet dangling over the sides, Daniel squinted up at the pale blue sky and watched the white fluffy clouds drift by overhead. "This is the life!"

"How lazy is this?" Beth sighed. "I could stay out here all da—" She never finished what she was saying. The dinghy lurched violently to one side, as if some huge weight had suddenly crashed down on it. Instantly they were catapulted into the icy cold water.

Beth's shriek of terror was the last sound Daniel heard before the water closed over his head and everything became a muffled, suffocating chaos of bubbles and frantic flaying arms and legs.

Although the water half blinded him, he could still make out Beth's petrified face through the stream of bubbles pouring from her mouth. Despite the numbing shock of the sudden cold, he managed to reach out and grab her. Desperately holding on to her, Daniel kicked out with his legs, pushing upwards, his lungs screaming out in agony. Beneath him, he caught something soft yet solid with his foot and pushed against it, speeding their ascent to the surface. But the water was being churned into a frenzy. Froth and bubbles and flashes of yellow swirled before him as he struggled towards the air.

Then, just as he broke the surface, something gripped him. A steely band clamped around his middle and he lashed out. Above the chaos came his dad's voice. "It's me, Daniel! I've got you! Calm down!"

Len was there too. He'd grabbed Beth. "I've got her! Let go of her now, Daniel. You're safe, Beth, don't panic, I've got you." Holding her head clear of the water, Len swam on his back towards shore.

"Can you swim with me, Daniel?" his dad asked, treading water as Daniel gulped in air.

"Yes," he spluttered, striking out through the icy grey water towards the shore. It seemed an eternity before they were finally in the shallows. Andrew helped Daniel wade out, while Len scooped Beth up in his arms and carried her. Finally they all collapsed onto the marshy grassland.

"Are you all right?" Andrew gasped, slapping Daniel on the back to help him breathe easier. And then, furiously, he exploded. "What the devil happened? I told you not to mess about! What were you playing at?"

"We didn't..." Daniel began, but there was water and weed in his mouth, and he coughed until he was sick.

"We weren't messing about!" Beth cried between spluttering and clinging onto her dad.

"Honest, Dad, we weren't doing anything," pleaded Daniel, wiping his eyes. "The dinghy just threw us out. It flipped and we were in the water. I don't know what happened. You've got to believe us!"

"I suppose it's possible the rope got snagged around something beneath the surface and caused them to flip over," Len suggested, moving Beth's bedraggled hair from her eyes.

"It must have," Daniel shivered, looking towards the loch, puzzled. All was calm now. The dinghy was floating serenely at the end of its rope. It was almost as if nothing had happened. Melissa came staggering up to them. She was red-faced and breathless. "Is everyone all right?" she gasped.

"They're okay," Daniel's dad assured her. "Don't ask me what happened..."

"Didn't you see?" she began. "It—"

"Scooby!" A cold hand had circled Daniel's heart, and squeezed until he cried out in agony. "Scooby!"

Staggering to his feet, he ran back into the water, scanning the surface frantically. Everyone else leaped into action too. But there was no sign of the puppy. Desperately, Daniel floundered through the mud and reeds, praying Scooby had made it to the shore, shouting her name at the top of his voice.

And then he recalled pushing against something solid and soft under water, and he prayed even harder. *Don't let that have been Scooby...please don't let that have been Scooby.*

Beth stood on the shore, crying, while the two

dads waded in, going deeper and deeper until they were swimming.

"Scooby!" Daniel yelled again, tears streaming down his cheeks. "Scooby! Where are you? Scooby!"

And then, suddenly, a familiar little *woof!*

They all heard, and everyone looked around frantically to see where the bark had come from.

"There she is!" Daniel whooped at the top of his voice. "She's still in the dinghy. Scooby! Stay there, we're coming. Don't move."

As the two dads struck out towards the dinghy to guide it in, Daniel and Beth hauled on the rope, bringing the craft to shore. As soon as it was close enough, Daniel's dad lifted the puppy from the boat and handed her to Daniel. He hugged her fiercely. "Scooby! I thought you'd drowned. I thought I'd lost you."

They all waded onto dry land. Daniel's dad put his arm around his son, and fussed Scooby. "I really don't know how you kids managed to fall in, but at least you're all safe and accounted for now!"

"What do you mean, they *fell* in?" asked Melissa incredulously. "They didn't just *fall* in at all."

"That's what we've been trying to tell them," wailed Daniel, amazed that she was on their side for once. "The dinghy just flipped us out."

"We'll have the inquest once we're out of these wet clothes," said Andrew, ushering them all back towards camp. "We'll all get pneumonia at this rate."

"It was the beast!" Melissa announced, stopping everyone dead in their tracks.

"What?" Andrew snapped.

"I came running when I saw you swimming out to the children," she said excitedly. "From where I was standing, I could see something else in the water, well, not exactly *see* it, just the disturbance it caused. There was something big thrashing about in the water with them. If only I'd had the camcorder ready..."

For a second, everyone fell silent. And then Beth screamed, "No!" and turned sobbing into her dad's arms.

"Now don't alarm yourself, Beth love," Len said softly, holding her close. But the look he exchanged with Andrew was brimming with questions. It was clear, however, that this wasn't the time to ask them. "Melissa's mistaken, love," he said softly, leading Beth away. "And everyone is fine, no one's hurt. What we need to do now, is get you into some dry clothes."

Heading off towards camp, he flashed another glance back – this time at Melissa, and Daniel couldn't help thinking, *if looks could kill...*

"I'm telling you it was the beast," Melissa said defensively, as soon as Len and Beth were out of earshot.

Andrew shook his head. "But couldn't you have waited until Beth was out of the way?"

"This is a monumental sighting," Melissa argued. "I told you we shouldn't have brought children along. If only I'd got the camcorder out in time, there'd be no argument then. And I have to say, Andrew, I don't think the children bumped into the beast by accident. This was a determined action on the beast's part."

Andrew's gaze hardened, reminding her that there was still a child present. "Melissa, we need to get into dry clothes. Whatever you've got to say can wait!"

But there was no stopping her. "It may have been dead for ten thousand years, but its predatory nature is still very much alive. You could tell by the determination and power in the disturbance it caused. Believe me, that beast was after its prey."

Already frozen to the bone from his soaking, Daniel felt an even icier chill. "And *we* were its prey? It was trying to kill us?"

"Not *all* of you. In fact, I think that most of us are of little interest to this spirit." Her eyes shifted in the direction of the puppy clutched in Daniel's arms. "But it's definitely interested in one of us."

"Who?" Daniel breathed, beginning to feel sick.

His dad's firm grip tightened on his shoulder, as he turned and steered Daniel back towards camp. "This is getting out of hand. We need to get dry...now!"

"Who?" Daniel shouted back as his dad led him away.

"The little dog, of course," Melissa called after them. "The beast is after your dog!"

chapter eight

"Daniel, you're not to take that literally," Andrew tried to explain as they squelched back into camp. "Melissa is being overly dramatic. She's excited and getting a bit carried away. Spirits have no physical substance. They certainly can't turn back into solid matter and come alive again."

Daniel was trembling, and not just with the cold. "What if they can?" he asked miserably.

"Your monitors keep showing paranormal readings when Scooby is around."

"Not at all," his dad argued reassuringly. "The first time anything odd registered, you and Scooby were off exploring some distance away. When it happened in the cave, Scooby was outside with Beth." He looked steadily at him. "Son, we have to face it, I do think there is some spirit activity going on here in the valley, but I don't think it's to do with a prehistoric animal coming back to life. That's illogical. I would even argue against this spirit belonging to an animal at all. In fact, there's a real difference of opinion amongst paranormal investigators as to whether animals have spirits. I personally think this phenomenon is the collective spirit energy from the men who died in battle."

"So why did I hear it roar?" Daniel asked unhappily.

"Battle cries could sound like a roar," he suggested. Then he added gently, "Son, I've been investigating the paranormal for nearly ten years, and I've never heard of any evidence of a spirit manifesting itself and coming back to life. Now let's hurry up and get dry. I don't know about you, but I'm perished!"

Wanting desperately to believe his dad, Daniel got dried and changed into some warm clothing, but his head was spinning, and thoughts were going crazy in his brain.

When everyone emerged from their tents, warm and dry, Andrew made hot drinks while Len rigged up a washing line for the sodden clothes. But Beth was far from happy.

"I want to go home!" she stated, as they sat with their mugs of hot chocolate. "I hate it here! I hate all this horrible ghostly stuff! I hate boats that turn upside down! And I hate nearly drowning!"

Melissa came out of her tent, notebook and pen in hand. "I'm afraid that's not an option for another day at least, my dear. Tomorrow is the anniversary of the Battle of Endrith, which we can't miss. It's one of the primary reasons we've all given up our time to be here."

"More ghosts!" Beth wailed. "Dad, I really,

really don't like it here. If it was the beast that tipped us up, that means it's real. And if it can overturn a boat, then it could really hurt us."

"That is *not* happening," warned Len, fixing them both with a steely look. "The only actual evidence we've got of anything supernatural are electromagnetic disturbances and temperature fluctuations. There's absolutely no evidence of manifestation."

Melissa threw her hands up in despair. "No evidence! Just how much evidence do you need? Aren't you forgetting the EVP readings, not to mention my extrasensory perception – and the boat! For heaven's sake, the boat! Oh I do wish I'd grabbed the camcorder when I saw what was happening. Like a fool, I just left everything and ran down to see if I could help. I was actually worried about the children!"

"While I appreciate your concern for the children," said Len, sounding quite exasperated, "I also wish you'd recorded the event. At least that might have helped settle the argument once and for all."

"There is no argument as far as I'm concerned," said Melissa, folding her arms. "There is poltergeist activity going on here, and the fact is, this spirit is gaining in strength and momentum."

Daniel stared at her, wishing he knew whether she was a true psychic or a complete nutter! "So, if it was the beast who tipped us into the water, what's to stop it ripping us to shreds?"

"Steady on, Daniel," began his dad, placing a calming hand on his shoulder. "That's not possible. As I tried to explain earlier, there's no physical substance to a spirit, it's purely an energy force. It can't summon up solid matter and come back to life."

Melissa clasped her hands together in glee. "I think you'll find that a lot of investigators believe they can. All we need is visual proof. If only I'd had the camcorder, what I witnessed would have turned the paranormal circles upside-down. Our society would be famous!"

"Except we'd all be dead!" Daniel shouted. "If the beast becomes real, then it's going to attack us and kill us."

"But it doesn't want us, it only wants the puppy," Melissa said unkindly.

"Now hang on," said Andrew. "Let's keep cool and talk a bit of sense. This is all getting too far-fetched. Everyone's imaginations are running wild."

Melissa blustered on, ignoring Andrew's warning look. "Oh, come on! You can't deny that the presence of the puppy is accentuating the situation." Melissa paused then shrieked, "I know! I have an idea!"

"I don't want to hear your stupid ideas," Daniel raged.

Melissa suddenly made a grab at Scooby, snatching her and holding her at arm's length above her head. Scooby gave a little squeal and wriggled frantically. "If my notions are stupid, you won't mind if we tie the dog to our recording equipment and see if the beast comes to investigate."

"Give her back!" Daniel yelled, horrified, leaping up to try and get Scooby off her.

Andrew was even more furious. He quickly retrieved Scooby from Melissa and placed her back in Daniel's arms. "What a callous, insensitive, ludicrous thing to suggest!"

Melissa instantly backed down. "Oh, for heaven's sake, I was only joking. Honestly, you're all getting so uptight! I was just having a little fun." She tried to stroke Scooby, but Daniel pulled back. "It was a joke!" she stressed again, looking offended. "Oh, for goodness' sake..." And throwing her hands in the air she strutted away, muttering about how some people had no sense of humour.

A cold, unfriendly atmosphere descended over the camp for the rest of the morning. Everyone sat quietly, reading or doing crosswords. Hardly anyone spoke. Melissa disappeared into her tent for hours, finally emerging to announce that she was going to investigate the cave again.

"Don't worry, I'll go alone," she said when no one moved. "I don't expect anyone will want to come with me anyway."

Len put aside his book and got to his feet. "I'll come. It's a bad idea going on your own. You might fall, or anything."

Beth jumped up and clung onto her dad's arm. "If you're going, I'm coming too!"

He smiled kindly. "Wouldn't you rather stay here with Daniel and Scooby?"

"No! I want to stay with you!" she said determinedly, hanging onto him.

"Okay, that's fine," Len agreed. "Actually, you could help with the camcorder. Do you fancy doing some filming?"

She brightened a little. "Really? You'll let me work the video camera?"

"It needs a very steady hand," said Len. "Think you're up to it?"

Her face lit up. "I'll try."

Daniel sat tight. Making a film would have been fun. Only there was no way he was going anywhere with the madwoman. He waited until they were well away before saying anything. "Dad, what do you reckon...really? Is there a ghost? Is it really after Scooby?"

His dad set aside his magazine and breathed a long drawn-out sigh. "There's nothing after your dog," he said. "Like I told you before, I do think there's some kind of paranormal entity, but it's probably the combined spirit entities of the Highlanders who died here. A lot of people have heard unusual sounds around the battle's anniversary. And, like it or not, Melissa has this sixth sense – she feels things we don't, so all this is affecting her more than the rest of us." He cast Daniel a wry smile. "But basically, she's spooking us all out."

"So, you're positive Scooby isn't in danger?" asked Daniel hopefully.

His dad smiled reassuringly at Daniel. "Do you honestly think we'd still be here if that was the case?"

Daniel had to agree, his dad wouldn't be putting their lives in danger. He glanced at Scooby. His puppy was back to her normal mischievous self, snuffling about in the long grass. "No, suppose not." Then he grinned. "Melissa's a complete nutter, isn't she?"

"I wouldn't go that far, son. Let's just say that she's melodramatic." He smiled again. "Fancy a spot of fishing? The rods are still down by the loch."

"Yeah, great!"

Sitting by the water, with the fishing lines stretched tight and Scooby exploring amongst the reeds, Daniel tried not to relive the awful sensation of being underwater, and the terrible moment he thought Scooby had drowned. Before it all happened the loch had been as calm as this – peaceful, tranquil, with just a light breeze playing across the surface.

Sitting quietly with his dad, Daniel studied the rippling pattern on the water, but the more he stared, the more he could see something odd about it. There was one patch of water that was making a strange V-shape...

His stomach gave a funny lurch. "What's making the water ripple like that, Dad?" He tried to sound calm and not give way to panic.

"Where, son?"

Daniel pointed. "There, see? Something's causing a wake."

His dad shielded his eyes. "Can't see anything myself. It's this sunlight, it creates strange effects."

But Daniel couldn't take his eyes off it. The

ripples were definitely forming in a V-shape, as if something was swimming this way. In fact, the more he looked, the more he thought he could see a shape sticking out above the water.

He jumped up and made a grab for Scooby, holding her close, despite her muddy paws going all over him. "Look...over there. There's something in the water! It's coming this way..."

"Now hang on, Daniel," said his dad calmly. "The only thing I can see is that old tree root floating out there. The breeze is probably changing the water direction around it."

Daniel was ready to run. His heart was pounding so fast, he felt sick. "You don't think it's a head...a big animal's head? You don't think it's something swimming?"

"No I don't, son." His dad smiled confidently, remaining relaxed in his fishing chair. "It's a tree root, and you're scaring yourself to death. Now sit down, check to see if you've caught anything – and for goodness' sake put Scooby down. Look at the state of your sweatshirt!"

Reluctantly, Daniel did as he was told.

Minutes ticked by and nothing loomed up at them from the depths of the loch. No beasts leaped out to drag Scooby off. And the tree root continued to drift lazily across the loch.

By the time they packed up, after catching just two little silvery fish, which they threw back, Daniel was beginning to relax. Things weren't as black as they seemed. It was purely people's imaginations running away with them.

And there certainly wasn't a dangerous sabre-toothed tiger after their blood.

It wasn't imagination that was causing the turmoil in the air on a rocky ledge near the base of Endrith Mountain. A vicious, snarling, spitting entity was growing in strength and fury.

With his back against the rock face, Karbel had been cornered by a male human.

He had been zigzagging his way down the mountain to try again to snatch his prey when, leaping onto a jutting ledge, he had come face-to-face with this human.

His hatred and anger flared. Humans were constantly thwarting his efforts to take the cub. Just like when he was mortal, when it had been a human who stood in his way of food – and had caused his death. How he detested humans.

Now he reacted naturally, as any wild beast would react when trapped.

He attacked!

With a mighty roar he lashed out with ferocious talons and deadly fangs. But his spirit form held no substance. His claws and teeth sliced through the air – through the male human – with no effect. The effort of trying to snatch the cub from the sailing vessel had drained him. All traces of mortality had slipped away from him again.

But as he roared and slashed through the air – cutting through this human – his frustration and rage grew. He wanted to slice this mortal into shreds. He snarled and bit and lashed out – but still the human refused to fall.

Instead he cried out in elation as he looked at the small weapon in his hand.

Karbel's fury exploded, and with his rage

came a brief flash of mortality. In one mighty surge, he lashed out with huge razor-sharp claws.

To his satisfaction the weapon spun from the human's hand and bounced all the way to the bottom of the mountain, scattering pieces in all directions. At the same instant the human clutched at his arm, where spots of red blood suddenly oozed.

Karbel sprang past him, bounding down the mountainside and streaking across the valley – away from these hated humans.

Daniel and his dad were back in camp sipping mugs of soup when they spotted the others returning. It was immediately obviously that something was wrong.

Len was clutching his arm. His shirt was stained red and he walked slowly, stumbling. Beth was at his side and Melissa came striding on ahead.

"Now what?" Daniel heard his dad murmur under his breath, as they hastily ran to meet them.

"We need the first-aid box," Melissa exclaimed, hurrying past.

"My dad's cut his arm!" Beth cried, her face crumpling as Daniel and his dad reached them.

"How did this happen, mate?" Andrew asked, remaining calm but placing his arm around Len's waist to support him.

"It's nothing, just a graze." Len dismissed Andrew's concern, although the paleness of his face said he was more hurt than he was letting on. "A couple of plasters should do the trick."

Andrew took a closer look and winced. "Daniel, run back and boil up the kettle. Beth, go with him and help Melissa find some bandages. The first-aid box is in the van."

"Is it bad?" Daniel asked, though he already knew the answer.

"Just do as you're told, son. Hurry up now."

Neither Daniel nor Beth was allowed to watch the clean-up operation, so they hung around outside Melissa's tent while Andrew patched Len up. Melissa, however, seemed more concerned about the broken monitor.

She sat puzzling, with the pieces spread all over the fold-up table. She called through the tent flaps, "Len, can you remember what the readings were on this ion detector before you dropped it?"

"Not exactly," Len replied, sounding exhausted. "It's all a bit of a jumble in my head. I remember the pointer shooting up the scale, next thing I knew I'd dropped the monitor and there was this incredible pain in my arm. I must have caught myself on a jagged rock."

"Well it was one sharp rock," remarked Andrew, as a moment later the two men emerged from the tent. "I hate to say this, mate, but while I've done a pretty neat patching-up job, you're going to need stitches in that – and a tetanus jab."

Horrified, Beth threw her arms around her dad's waist. "You're not going to hospital, are you, Dad?"

"Well, I'm up to date with my tetanus," said Len, glancing at Andrew. "It doesn't really need stitches, does it?"

"I'm pretty sure it does."

Beth started to cry.

Len hugged her with his good arm. "Hey, it's okay. I'll be back before you know it, good as new. Melissa, you can drive me, can't you? I can't manage it one-handed and it would be better if Andrew stopped here with the kids."

"Me?" she exclaimed. "But I don't drive! I thought you knew that."

The two dads glanced at each other. Then Andrew said stiffly, "No, we didn't know that."

"I'll manage," said Len. "I could take the sling off..."

"No way!" Andrew stated flatly. "You're not driving yourself with that injury. Plus you've lost a fair bit of blood. We don't want you blacking out on these roads. I'll drive and we'll all go."

"We can't all go off and leave our equipment and everything," frowned Melissa. "And it's the anniversary of the battle tonight. I can't possibly miss that or this whole trip will have been pointless. I'll stay!"

Andrew rubbed his chin. "On your own? No, I don't think so, Melissa. It's far too isolated for a woman on her own."

"Nonsense! I'll be fine... I know what! I'll keep the little dog with me. She can guard me..."

"No!" Daniel interrupted. There was no way he was going to leave Scooby with her. "You'll be busy, you might not notice if she wanders off."

"Of course I'd notice. I'll take excellent care of her," Melissa argued, stooping down to fuss the puppy. "Besides, you won't be allowed to take dogs into the hospital and you can't keep her cooped up alone in the van for hours on end."

Andrew glanced at him. "She's right, son. She'd be better off here."

"Well I'll stay too!" Daniel announced determinedly.

For a second he thought he glimpsed a flash of annoyance cross Melissa's face, but then she clasped her hands together in delight.

"That's marvellous. Thank you, young man. I won't be in the least worried now with you *and* a guard dog to protect me."

Andrew got his jacket. "Well, if you're sure, son, we'd better set off now. With any luck, we'll be back before it gets dark, so at least I'll be around for the vigil later."

Half an hour later they were all set to go. After watching everyone board the van, Daniel stood waving as the vehicle wove its way across the valley and finally ascended the hill that led to the road.

With a final wave from Beth, the van disappeared from view. Sighing, Daniel turned around, expecting Scooby to be at his side.

Instead, his puppy was nestled in Melissa's arms. She was stroking her and softly whispering in her ear. Talking so softly that Daniel couldn't hear what she was saying.

He instantly reached out to retrieve his pet. "She needs her dinner."

For a second, Melissa was reluctant to let her go. Then she handed her back, and smiled. But it was a cold smile that failed to reach her eyes.

chapter nine

"Now, how shall we entertain ourselves until they all get back?" Melissa asked casually, as she buttered some bread for a sandwich.

"I dunno," Daniel murmured, feeling edgy and uncomfortable with just Melissa for company. He almost wished now that he'd gone with the others, although he wouldn't have left Scooby. He glanced at his watch. They'd only been gone a quarter of an hour. It was going to be a long evening. "How long do you think they'll be?"

"Five or six hours at the least," Melissa answered, opening a tin of tuna. "It's five o'clock now. I imagine they'll be back by midnight anyway."

It seemed an eternity away. "I think I'll go and read my book," said Daniel.

"Wouldn't you rather do some camcording? You could take over where Beth left off. She was doing an excellent job – I'm sure you could too."

Daniel hesitated, even though he really quite fancied having a go with the video camera. "I'm not taking Scooby near that cave again."

"No, no, we'll stay well away from there," Melissa assured him. "I really wanted to record those places associated with the Battle of Endrith. I intend putting together a documentary for the society's annual meeting. You could be credited as assistant cameraman if you do a good job."

It didn't sound too awful an idea, and at least it would help pass the time. Taking a bite of his sandwich, Daniel shrugged. "Okay!"

"Excellent!" She beamed, putting down her sandwich and bustling around getting all the gear together again. "Bring your dog's lead."

"She doesn't need it. She just hangs around with me."

"I'd be happier," Melissa said, looking earnestly at Daniel. "The last thing we want is to lose track of your dog after everything else that's happened."

She had a point. It would be too easy to take his eye off Scooby if he was concentrating on filming.

After they'd finished eating, they set off towards the narrowest part of the valley – a lush green strip between the edge of the loch and the forest.

"This is where the battle is supposed to have taken place," Melissa said, after giving Daniel instructions on how to use the camcorder. He practised on Scooby, zooming in and out as she sniffed around the edges of the forest.

"Not too far, Scooby!" Daniel called, busily adjusting his camera angle.

"Put the dog on her lead, dear," Melissa suggested. "Hook it round a branch. It's an extending lead, so she'll still be able to explore, but at least she can't get far."

"Yeah, okay," Daniel agreed, clipping the lead to his pet's collar, and hooking the loop around a low branch. "Be good, Scooby, I won't be long."

Scooby sat, tail wagging uncertainly. And then she yapped.

Daniel ruffled her ears. "I'm not going far. Don't worry!"

"Now then, Daniel, I'd like you to film this area," suggested Melissa. "Including the loch and amongst the trees. Make it interesting, use the zoom and the wide angle." She smiled. "You're the cameraman. Be artistic!"

Scooby continued barking and Daniel looked back, watching everything through the viewfinder of the video camera.

"She'll be fine," Melissa assured him, rummaging through her holdall for her equipment. "You just concentrate on filming."

Already imagining his name being credited as

cameraman on this documentary Melissa was making, Daniel sought out the most picturesque and interesting angles – and tried not to let Scooby's constant yapping disturb him.

The cub's cries echoed across the valley. Karbel's spirit form loped through the marshland at the edge of the loch, ears attuned to the sound of its yelping. Quickening his pace, lengthening his stride, Karbel's great paws began to pound through the shallow water. If anyone had been watching they probably would have put the tide of ripples down to a strong breeze blowing across the loch.

The cub's yapping continued...

Karbel bounded faster, picking up on the scent of the cub. And then his yellow cat eyes spotted the small creature. It had been captured. It was tied by the neck to a bush, struggling and crying to be free.

Any predator could take the cub. It was too easy...it was the work of humans...

His hatred for them grew. A furious mist glazed his eyes and the shallow waters of the loch began dancing in waves all along the shoreline, as if a storm was blowing up.

Karbel thundered on, his hatred of humans almost overshadowing his desire to taste flesh. Almost, but not quite...

Now if anyone had seen, they'd have known no wind could disturb the water this way. This disturbance was unnatural – caused by something that moved with determination, growing in strength and momentum...and visibility.

Karbel's shimmering glass-like body merged with the grey waters of the loch behind him, yet for anyone intent on looking, they couldn't have missed seeing his great long curved back and rounded belly, those massive sturdy legs and paws – and his immense, grotesque head with its long vicious fangs that defied anything to get in its way.

The cub remained tethered, struggling and calling out. Karbel moved swiftly.

The cub glanced his way, and for a few panic-stricken seconds pulled frantically against its tether

– wrenching its neck, bending the branch that held it fast.

Karbel sank low on his belly, eyes alert, senses acute, aware of the humans nearby. He must never underestimate them. They once took his life. They could have the power to take his spirit. He had to move swiftly.

He crept forward until the smell of the cub's fear filled his nostrils. The small creature ceased its crying and flattened itself to the ground. As Karbel sprang, it rolled in submission onto its back, baring its soft underbelly to his fangs.

It was shadowy amongst the trees. The sun, beginning to set low in the sky, sent brilliant shafts of light through the leafy branches, so that everywhere was streaked in light and shade.

Daniel concentrated hard, hoping his filming would look atmospheric. Being a cameraman might not be a bad job, when he was older. Turning, he retraced his steps into the open valley and panned the camera out across the loch with the magnificent mountain as its background. He hoped it would look as dramatic as he'd intended.

Sweeping the camcorder round, Melissa appeared through the viewfinder. He focused on her, surprised to see that she too was filming, or at least fiddling with her camcorder. She was half hidden behind a tree. He watched her through the viewfinder. She seemed to be having trouble with her equipment.

Wondering what she was intending to film, he lowered his camera so that he could see the whole area again. At the same moment, he realized that Scooby wasn't barking. Then he saw why – and his heart missed a beat. His pet was flat on her back again, the lead stretched tight.

But Daniel couldn't see clearly – there was a strange mist surrounding Scooby. He rubbed his eyes, but the mist remained. It was like a heat haze, quivering, shimmering. But it was only in one place. It wasn't his eyes playing tricks on him – he could see everything else perfectly clearly. The misty haze was only around his pet.

He took a few stumbling steps forward, barely able to believe what he was seeing. It was a great mass of light, shimmering and moving. It had no exact shape...until suddenly, in a split second, the mist shifted and to Daniel's horror he saw the distinct, terrifying shape of an animal...

A huge creature. A creature from some other time, some other place – not of this earth, not of this lifetime.

The beast!

With a shriek, Daniel broke into a run. With no thought for his own safety, he charged at the shimmering light looming over his dog, shouting and screaming for it to leave her alone. Stumbling, blind with shock, sick with fear, Daniel ran as fast as his legs would take him, desperate to reach his pet.

Suddenly, the beast took Scooby by the scruff of the neck and lifted her clean off the ground, dragging twigs and leaves from the bush as it tore the lead free.

"No! Leave her alone!" he shrieked as the little puppy dangled in mid-air, locked in the jaws of this monstrous apparition, helpless...pitifully helpless.

Scooby was suddenly swung around, and Daniel glimpsed the look of terror on his pet's little face – and the shimmering feline eyes above her that glinted with determination. And then, in one great bound, the ghostly beast sprang away, with Scooby still dangling from its jaws.

"No!" Daniel screamed, charging at the mass of light as it shot past him, blasting him with heat. "No! Let her go!"

A short distance away, the beast stopped and, as if toying with the puppy, turned its massive head so that Scooby swung pathetically from its jaws.

With a sob, Daniel sprinted towards them again, but the beast turned and broke into an effortless run, taking its prize further and further away. Its gait seemed almost proud – loping away with Scooby in its mouth like a trophy.

With his face wet with tears, Daniel chased after them, but the beast gathered speed. Daniel couldn't catch up. No matter how fast he ran, no matter that his lungs were bursting, and his legs cried out for him to stop, he couldn't catch up with the beast, and his dog.

All he could do was watch in horror as Scooby dangled in mid-air, swaying helplessly, disappearing further and further into the distance, far across the valley. Until finally, he couldn't see the mass of shimmering light at all, and Scooby was just a speck in the distance.

And then she was gone.

chapter ten

"Daniel! Daniel, are you all right?" Melissa was bending over him as he lay exhausted amongst the purple heather, blinded by tears.

He lashed out at her, arms flailing. "It was a trick! You tricked me...you used Scooby as bait, and it worked. The beast's got her. I hate you! I hate you! I hate you!"

She dodged his flaying arms. Her face was

flushed with running halfway across the valley after him. "I didn't mean for her to run away. She'll come back. We'll find her."

He stared at her through his tears as if she was stupid. "She didn't *run* off! The beast snatched her up in its mouth – you must have seen. You were there!"

For a second, a stunned look flashed across her face. "The beast? It came? You saw it?"

"Are you blind?" Daniel raged. "How could you have missed it? That huge ugly thing, shimmering like glass."

Flabbergasted, she ran her fingers through her hair. "I don't believe this! I'd have got all that on film if my camcorder hadn't started playing up. I heard you shouting about something, but I'd just sat myself down on a tree stump to try putting new batteries in the thing." She shook her head. "I can't believe it – I missed all that!" She grabbed Daniel's arms then. "So you saw it? You actually saw the beast? What was it like, was it big—"

"Get off me!" he shouted. "You're evil! You knew the beast would come if you lured it with bait. You used my dog as bait." His voice cracked. "Poor Scooby...I've got to find her, it might not be too late..."

Daniel stumbled to his feet and took off in the direction he had last seen Scooby being carried, towards the mountain...maybe the cave.

"Daniel, come back here! You can't just go running off, you'll get lost!" Melissa was following, but even though he was exhausted, he could still outrun her.

The sun was sinking lower, dipping into the loch, transforming the grey waters into a lake of gold and amber. The mountain loomed. Now Daniel saw how many shadowy ridges and crevices there were. His pet could have been dragged into any one of them.

Scooby could already be dead.

He'd seen enough wildlife programmes on the television. He'd seen lions and tigers attacking their prey, savaging and devouring it. His throat tightened and tears flooded his eyes. He wiped them away quickly. He needed to be able to see clearly. Scooby was here somewhere.

He cupped his hands around his mouth and shouted at the top of his voice, "Scooby! Scooby, where are you?"

He listened. Standing stock-still, he heard the faint echo of his voice drifting across the valley. And then silence. Total, utter, absolute silence.

No familiar, excited little yap. Nothing.

He stumbled on, clambering over chunks of granite rock to reach the cave they'd thought was the beast's lair. He'd thought Melissa was crazy when they'd been there before. But the beast probably *was* hiding in the shadows. A chill ran down Daniel's spine as he recalled how frightened Scooby had been. Had his pet sensed the beast then?

Dogs can be sensitive to the supernatural, Melissa had said.

Was that why she'd been so desperate to escape? So desperate that she'd scratched Beth.

Unless it hadn't been Scooby who'd scratched her at all...

Daniel reached the gaping black chasm in the mountainside, and stood there, shivering. "Scooby...

Scooby, here, matey..." His voice was quivering. His whole body was trembling. What if the beast was there, watching him through those sharp feline eyes? Slinking up on him, about to use those sabre teeth.

What if Scooby was just a pile of bones on the cave floor...what if *he* was about to be the beast's next victim? It would be ravenous, waking up after thousands of years of sleep – one small puppy might not be enough to satisfy its hunger.

His foot hit something. Almost too afraid to look down in case it was Scooby's body, he saw to his relief that it was only the bit of wood he'd picked up the other day. It wasn't much of a weapon, but he grasped it anyway and slowly, warily, inched into the black cavern.

His feet shuffled across the dusty cave floor while his eyes tried to adjust to the gloom. Although he was shivering, it wasn't because of the cold. In fact the cave seemed to have retained some of the heat from the day's sunshine. It lacked the icy chill he now associated with something supernatural hovering there.

But Scooby wasn't there either.

Daniel hurried back outside only to spot Melissa coming his way. He dipped out of sight behind a rock. She'd try and drag him back, and he needed to search for Scooby quickly. Although, deep down, he feared it was already too late.

Karbel moved with stealth and agility, adrenalin coursing through his body after catching his prey. Easy though it was, hunting was still a source of immense excitement. Now his prize dangled from his jaws – a small, wriggling cub.

As Karbel picked his way from ridge to ridge, climbing higher, he felt the warmth from its breathing body. He felt the softness of its fur. For a moment he was reminded of something. Something so long ago, so deep in the recesses of his memories, it was almost irretrievable – but not quite.

Memories of his mother carrying him by the scruff. For an instant, the smell, softness and warmth of the cub reminded him of playful tussles with his siblings and the pleasure of companionship, something he had experienced so little of in life – and in death.

The pup was a light weight dangling from his massive jaws, and as Karbel sprang effortlessly on from ridge to ridge, lost in his memories, the swaying cub caught a glancing blow against a rock and squealed in pain.

Daniel searched for hours – until the sun set and the stars came out. The Highlands were immense, vast swathes of mountain and valley and dense forest. He knew he was lost. He knew he'd never find his way back to camp. Time after time he tried to get a signal on his mobile phone, but the gigantic mountains blocked off any links with the world beyond them, and silence wrapped itself around his head like a suffocating pillow.

Only his voice as he called out Scooby's name, time after time, shattered the silence. Now he was hoarse from shouting and his ears hurt with the strain of listening for his pet's familiar yapping.

He'd long lost track of Melissa. She would

have returned to the camp ages ago. Vaguely Daniel wondered if the others were back yet. His dad would be frantic, but there was nothing he could do about that. He didn't know the way back.

He didn't want to go back. How could he leave Scooby out here, alone with that monster? Although, what chance was there of Scooby being alive now?

He was too exhausted, too cold and thirsty to cry. He trudged on, stumbling through the blackness, tripping and falling so many times his jeans were in tatters. He had no idea of the time. Two, three in the morning maybe. It was too dark to see his watch.

Then he heard something through the silence. A voice – someone calling his name. It was faint, a long way off, but definitely someone calling out to him. It sounded like his dad.

"Dad!" he yelled back, his voice cracking. "Over here!"

"Daniel!" The voice returned louder, elated. "Daniel, stay right where you are. Keep shouting. I'll find you."

He did as he was told, hopeful now that together they would find Scooby. He kept calling out, until finally he saw a beam of torchlight, and his dad emerged through the darkness, stumbling towards him.

Moments later he was being hugged fiercely. "Daniel, don't you ever go off like that again. We've all been frantic."

"I'm sorry, but I couldn't just leave Scooby with the beast, could I?"

"What are you talking about?" asked Andrew, holding Daniel at arm's length – and then hugging him again. "Never mind, let's get you back before hypothermia sets in."

"The beast took Scooby. It carried her off in its jaws, like a cat with a kitten," Daniel explained, then saw the look of disbelief on his dad's face. "Melissa did tell you what happened, didn't she?"

"Yes, she said that Scooby ran off and you'd gone searching for her."

"No!" Daniel gasped, horrified, pulling free. "That's not what happened at all! She tricked me into tying Scooby up. Then the beast came and snatched her."

"Daniel, you're exhausted, you've walked for ages. Come on, let's get you back. We'll look for Scooby in the morning. She's probably curled up asleep under some bush, you'll see. She wouldn't have wandered this far anyway. She may even be back at the tent. Did you think to check there, before wandering off?"

"Melissa's lied to you!" Daniel cried. "You've got to believe me, the beast came. I saw it! It took Scooby!"

"If that was so, wouldn't Melissa be wild with excitement?"

"No, because *she* didn't actually see the beast – I did. Anyway she's feeling really guilty about using Scooby as bait. She knows you'd be furious with her."

Andrew put his arm around Daniel's shoulder. "Come on, we'll sort this out in the morning, when you've rested."

By the time they reached camp, Daniel had repeated his story a hundred times, and his dad still didn't seem convinced.

Len and Beth were waiting. Len, with his arm in a sling, folded a blanket around Daniel, while a red-eyed Beth threw her arms around him.

"Is Scooby here?" Daniel asked, hoping against hope. Beth shook her head sadly.

"We'll organize a proper search tomorrow, first thing after breakfast. We'll call in mountain rescue if need be," promised Andrew, making hot chocolate for everyone.

"Where's Melissa?" Daniel demanded, glancing around.

"She's down at the battle site," Len replied. "It's the anniversary – the main reason she's here. And to give her her due, she did say she'd keep an eye out for you and Scooby."

"She can't face me. That's why she's not here!" Daniel said angrily.

"Why can't she face you?" Len said, puzzled.

"Because she tricked me into tying Scooby up and using her as bait to lure the beast," Daniel explained. "And it worked. The beast came and carried poor Scooby off."

Beth gasped while Len instinctively clutched at

his arm, as if something had just occurred to him about his accident. Softly, he remarked, "That's not how she explained things to us!"

Andrew handed out mugs of hot chocolate. "We'll get to the bottom of this in the morning. Right now, you kids need to get some sleep. So drink this and get to bed."

Beth took Daniel's hand. "You can drink yours in my tent, if you like."

Nodding unhappily, Daniel followed Beth into her tent, where they sat with blankets wrapped around them, leaving the adults to talk outside.

"No one believes me," murmured Daniel. "I don't suppose you do either."

She inched closer to him. "Tell me again, exactly what happened."

Wearily, Daniel explained how Melissa had got him to tie Scooby up, then kept him busy filming, and how he saw a shimmering image of the beast which had carried Scooby away in its mouth. He half expected Beth to laugh.

Instead, she sat wide-eyed and horrified. "Did Melissa see all this?"

Daniel shook his head. "She was fiddling with the camcorder and missed it all. She believes me though."

"Then why isn't she here on your side, making our dads believe you?"

"Because she knows they'll be mad at her for setting Scooby up as bait for the beast."

"Oh! That woman is hateful!" Beth declared angrily, but then her chin crumpled. "Oh, poor Scooby. Poor, poor Scooby. Will the beast...*hurt* her, do you think?"

Daniel shrugged, unable to speak as his eyes filled with tears again.

Beth wrapped her arms around him. "Oh, Daniel, what are we going to do?"

He rubbed his hands roughly over his eyes. "Well I'm not sitting doing nothing, that's for certain."

Beth stared at him. "What do you mean?"

He didn't answer as just then Len poked his head through the tent flap. "Kids, if you're both okay, Andrew and I are going to take a walk down to the battle site and have a word with Melissa.

Will you be all right?"

"Yeah, we'll be okay. I'm going to bed in a minute anyway," Daniel replied, forcing a yawn.

"Good man. Now don't you worry, we'll find Scooby in the morning, you'll see."

Andrew looked in then. "Feeling any better, son?"

He nodded. "I just want to go to bed, really."

"Yes, get some sleep. I'll try not to wake you when I get back."

Daniel nodded, and quietly sipped his drink as the two dads got their ghostbusting gear together. As soon as they'd gone, he scrambled to his knees and peered out of the tent.

"They've gone. But if they think I'm waiting till morning, with Scooby out there with that beast, they're mad."

"You're going out again," Beth murmured.

"I won't go too far, I promise. I'm not going to get lost again," said Daniel, turning back to Beth. "If you think about it, this valley seems to be where the beast has been hanging around. Maybe it doesn't go far either."

"The cave!" Beth suggested, excitedly. "Maybe it's taken Scooby to that cave."

"I've looked there, but I'll look again."

Beth threw the blanket off her. "Well you're not going alone this time. I'm coming with you!"

"Your dad will go mad."

She pulled on her coat then stuffed one of the pillows inside her sleeping bag. "He'll think I'm asleep when he looks in. You do the same, Daniel...Hurry up! Scooby needs us!"

He admired Beth's determination, but as Daniel returned to his tent for more warm clothes and a torch, and moulded his sleeping bag to look as if he was inside it, he had the most awful sinking feeling that it was already far too late to find his puppy alive.

Karbel was relishing the feeling of having a living creature so close to him. It had been thousands of years since another warm, breathing animal had stood beside him.

Inquisitively, Karbel moved his great head towards the cub, breathing in its scent, nuzzling its soft, furry body. It was trembling, fearful – it reminded Karbel of when he had been a young cub. He would have been this age when his whole family had been wiped out, leaving him orphaned and alone.

Karbel had known real fear as he'd watched his family trampled into the ground. He'd trembled pitifully, just as this cub trembled now.

The beast stood over the cub, sensing how its tiny heart was thudding with terror. Karbel understood its fear, felt at one with its solitude. Lowering his head he nudged the cub again, tucking it beneath his mighty front legs, sheltering it from the wind. The desire to savage the cub, to tear it to shreds and devour it, had melted away.

This creature was not food. What need had he of food anyway? This small creature was companionship – a friend. A friend to remain with him for all eternity, here in his valley.

But this could not be, not while they existed in two opposing states: Karbel in spirit form, rapidly losing all traces of mortality, and this cub, mortal and alive.

They were on different planes.

There was only one way to ensure the union would last for all time. And that was to strike through the heart of the cub. To stop that heart from beating. To sever its mortal coil and bring the cub into his world as a spirit.

The shimmering form of the beast looked down at the cub. Fear was clouding its brown eyes as it looked pitifully up at him.

He would be swift, the pain would be brief. He had no wish to make the cub suffer. Just one sharp stab through the heart with his fangs and it would be over. The cub's spirit would be released and Karbel would have companionship for ever more.

Opening his jaws wide, Karbel brought down the full force of his spirit onto the cub's small body.

The cub squealed, but it was only through fright. Once again, it seemed that all mortality had drained from Karbel. His physical frame had faded into insignificance. The cub's presence had calmed him. The absence of humans to bother him had removed the fury which had brought about his manifestation. For now, tranquil peacefulness had settled over him again.

But he would wait, bide his time and rest a while until he was ready to summon up the feelings needed to bring himself once more to full manifestation.

And once his strength and physical form were back, he would carry out the deed. And the cub's spirit would be his.

For now, Karbel's spirit rested on the rocky platform. He lay his sabre-toothed head close to the cub. For now, this would do – and his spirit rested where total peace and contentment reigned.

As the last strands of the beast's visibility dissolved into oblivion, Scooby shivered.

The body warmth from the strange and terrifying creature that had towered over her a second ago had dissolved to emptiness, and a cold, stark wind had taken its place, ruffling the fur of the frightened puppy. Shakily, Scooby staggered to her feet, and turned her head into the wind. A harsh, chilling blast flattened her ears to her head and tore into her trembling body. She stood shivering as the moonlight cast its silvery glow over the earth. From here Scooby could see the loch covered in a grey swirling mist. She could see the sweep of black valley, and silhouetted treetops against a backcloth of grey clouds.

She could see the whole world from up here... on this ledge, hundreds of metres up the side of the mountain face. As the wind cut into her again, threatening to blow her off the ridge, Scooby looked out from her solitary platform at the dark and shadowy domain stretched below her...and whined pitifully.

chapter eleven

Daniel and Beth crept out of their tent, keeping low as they ran stealthily across the dew-soaked grass.

An early morning mist swirled across the valley, like a blanket of fallen cloud laying ghostlike over the loch.

"What's that?" Beth suddenly hissed.

Daniel heard it too. It was faint, coming from

near the forest. Voices – Melissa's and his dad's. She sounded distressed.

Beth grabbed Daniel's arm. "It's Melissa! What's wrong with her?"

"Our dads are with her, she'll be all right," Daniel said dismissively, desperately wanting to get on.

"But why is she sobbing like that?"

"I don't care!" Daniel hissed back, but he found he was curious, and stood for a moment longer, listening.

"Clansmen, hundreds of them..." Melissa could vaguely be heard, as if she were describing a scene of horror. "Swords...can't you hear the clash? Can't you see the tartan?"

And then came the soothing tone of his dad's voice. Daniel couldn't hear what he said, but could guess. Melissa was having another melodramatic moment, and his dad and Len would be calming her down.

Only now, Daniel guessed that she probably *was* experiencing something paranormal. She wasn't a nutter like he'd thought. Somehow it would have been better if she was.

"Do you think she's seeing ghosts?" Beth asked, her eyes luminous in the first grey light of dawn.

"Probably," he murmured. "Come on, we need to get going."

By the time they reached the base of Endrith Mountain, the dawn chorus was just beginning, and the first grey light of daybreak was creeping over the horizon.

They didn't speak a single word until they reached the area where the ground rose and boulders littered their way. Daniel's stomach felt tied up in knots. What chance had they of finding Scooby alive?

He led the way, helping Beth over the rocks. Then she hung onto his arm as they stood hesitantly in the black cave mouth.

"Are we going in?" she breathed.

"You stay out here, I'll go in," said Daniel, but he didn't object when she followed him, still clinging onto his jacket.

Cautiously, he took a wary step and softly

called to his pet. "Scooby...Scooby, are you there? Here, girl!"

Again, only silence greeted him. He shone his torch around the cave floor, terrified that he might find a small pile of bones. He felt almost sick with relief when he found nothing.

"She's not here," he breathed at last.

"Would you live in a cave, Daniel?" Beth asked suddenly. "If you were a ghost and you could live anywhere you liked, would you really choose a cold, dark hole in a rock?"

He stared at her through the gloom. Then slowly, he stepped outside the shadowy confines of the cave and raised his face to the sky. The sheer magnificence of the towering mountain stretched way above him.

"Up there!" he breathed. "That's where I'd live, where you can see for ever!"

"Me too," Beth murmured. "Me too."

Darkness was lifting. Red streaks of light were banishing the grey, transforming the black sky into a glorious pink and golden sheen.

They retraced their steps, clambering around

the rocks at the base of the mountain, slipping on damp stone, sliding on dew-soaked moss, calling out Scooby's name as they went, constantly peering upwards.

Daniel wondered if they'd been missed yet back at camp. Although what did it matter? The only thing that mattered was finding his dog...but he still doubted that it would ever happen.

Some pebbles skittered down the mountainside nearby, and Daniel and Beth stopped and looked up. Judging by all the rocks littered around, rockfalls were fairly commonplace. If something fell now, they wouldn't stand a chance.

"Careful, Beth." Daniel held her back as he stepped forward. He couldn't tell where the pebbles had come from. It could have been any of the ridges or ledges that jutted out from this part of the mountain. They were almost like giant stairs, zigzagging their way upwards.

With daylight spreading over the valley, it was becoming easier to see shapes and colours...and suddenly Daniel could see something that was golden brown, the exact same colour as Scooby, dangling over a jutting ledge way, way above him.

"What's that?" he breathed, grabbing Beth's hand.

"What?"

"There," he said, pointing upwards. "There! Look, that ledge! See! *That* one. There's something moving...looks like a tail!"

Beth uttered a little cry and clung onto him. "It can't be...how could she get so far up the mountain?"

"The beast took her... It's her, isn't it! It is! I've got to get her."

"You can't," Beth cried. "You can't climb all the way up there, it's too dangerous."

"But I have to, she might fall."

As he eagerly started to climb, Beth pulled him back. "Daniel, wait!"

"Why? I need to get Scooby down."

"Look at her," Beth demanded, making him stop and take notice of her. And then more softly, she said, "*Look at her.*"

Daniel stood back a little and stared upwards. Scooby wasn't moving. Her little body lay motionless on the very edge of the ridge, as still as death.

"No..." Daniel uttered, as reality dawned and he sank to his knees. "We're too late, we're too late."

Beth sank down beside him, holding him tight. "You've done your best, Daniel. You can't risk climbing up there, if she's dea—"

"Oh, Scooby!" Daniel cried, his heart broken into a million pieces. "Scooby, I'm sorry, I'm so sorry..."

Then suddenly they heard a faint, but so familiar little *yap!*

"Scooby?" Daniel breathed, hardly daring to look in case it was just wishful thinking. But slowly he raised his head, and saw to his utter joy, a little golden-brown puppy standing there, on the edge, peering down. He jumped to his feet and punched the air.

"Yeah! Yeah, Scooby!" Daniel yelled, grabbing Beth and giving her a massive hug. "She's alive! She's okay!" He joined his hands as if in prayer. "Thank you, thank you, thank you!"

He swung Beth around and when they'd stopped spinning, announced, "I've got to get her down."

"How are you going to get up there?" Beth exclaimed, staring upwards. "Shall I run back and get our dads?"

As she spoke a tiny avalanche of pebbles skittered down the rock face as Scooby tried to scramble her way down off the rocky ledge.

"No! Stay, Scooby! Stay, girl!" Daniel yelled. He turned to Beth. "I need to get her now, before she falls. It'll be okay," he promised, seeing her anxious face. "See, there's ridges zigzagging upwards. I can do it – honest, I can."

Her face creased into a frown. "Well, please be careful, Daniel. Be really, really careful."

Studying the rock face, Daniel planned his route from ridge to ridge. It didn't look too difficult if you took it by stages. "I'm coming to get you, Scooby," he yelled up. "You stay right where you are and don't move!"

But the excited puppy was as anxious to get to Daniel as he was to reach her, and again tried to find a way off the ledge.

"No, stay, Scooby!" Beth shouted up. "Oh, Daniel, she's going to fall, I know it..."

"Stay, girl," Daniel repeated, as he hauled himself up from one ledge to the next. "I'm coming."

The mountain was so craggy that there were lots of footholds and he made good progress. It wasn't long before he was way above Beth's head. She stood, looking anxiously up, her hands clasped tightly together.

He climbed on, worried by Scooby's keenness to reach him. "I'm coming, girl. I can't be any quicker."

The higher he climbed, the colder the wind blew, and each time he glanced down, his head swam, making him cling to the rock face for support. It was a massive drop to the rocky ground below him now, and Beth looked tiny.

His hands were freezing and scratched, and his limbs hurt from the exertion of climbing. He stopped for breath, pressing himself against the rock face in case the dizziness returned.

But it was a fantastic view. From here he

could look out over the whole of the valley, and even their camp. There was no sign of movement. They must have gone to bed at last, exhausted after their eventful night. At least he and Beth hadn't been missed.

Continuing his climb, he saw that Scooby was only a few ridges above him now. So long as his nerve held out, he'd be there in a few minutes.

But it was so high. From a distance he guessed he would look like a fly on a wall. His dad would go berserk if he saw him now.

He tried to blank out thoughts about height and falling, even though the icy wind told him he was up where eagles soared. He concentrated on his pet, and getting her safely down. He'd tuck her inside his jacket and pull the drawstrings really tight, so she couldn't fall out.

He glanced up again, and saw Scooby peering over the ledge, her little tongue lolling out. "Hold on, girl, I'm coming. Don't move, okay? Stay right there, I'll be with you in a few minutes." Daniel kept on talking, not just to reassure his pet, but also to calm his own jangling nerves.

"Daniel!" Beth screamed out his name. It was so sudden and so intense, he almost stumbled.

"Don't do that!" he yelled down.

"Daniel, be careful!" she screamed again.

"I am being careful..."

"The beast!" she shrieked – so loudly that a hawk suddenly took flight from a crevice, spreading its beautiful brown wings and soaring effortlessly into the air.

Daniel clung onto a chunk of rock, his knuckles turning white, as cold fear turned him rigid. "What?"

"On the ridge where Scooby is!" she shrieked. "It's there! It's right beside Scooby. Daniel, I can see it. It's real... It's like glass, all shimmering. I can see through it, but I can make out its shape... its fangs. Oh Daniel, it's snarling and spitting...it looks so angry..."

Looking up, Daniel could still only see Scooby, but her little ears were now flattened to her head and fear clouded her eyes.

"It's manifesting itself, Daniel," Beth cried. "It's getting clearer, it's becoming real."

Daniel gritted his teeth. He'd come this far and he wasn't going back without his pet. "I'm coming, Scooby, you just hang on in there." He pulled himself up to the next ridge. One more ledge and he'd be able to reach up and grab her, beast or no beast.

He made it to the next level and stretched up...

"Daniel, no!" Beth screamed.

"It's okay, I can reach her," Daniel shouted, but as he moved to grab her, a massive shimmering apparition suddenly loomed up behind his pet, framing Scooby in a glowing luminescence.

Daniel staggered as Beth's scream rang out across the valley. Frantically he clawed at the rock face, clutching at the rough granite to steady himself.

The immense phantom presence of the huge beast gazed down at him, its massive head made grotesque by the two deadly fangs that protruded from its mouth. Yellow cat eyes shone with an unearthly glow. And between its front paws, a petrified puppy dog cowered and whimpered.

Daniel shrank down in sheer terror, shaking uncontrollably.

"It's real!" Beth shrieked from way, way below. "Daniel, watch out, it could kill you!"

He knew that. This beast had roamed the earth when dinosaurs and woolly mammoths inhabited the planet. It was so powerful that its spirit had survived for thousands of years. Daniel knew he was no match for its strength and power and viciousness.

The beast was manifesting itself more with every passing second. Now Daniel could see its colourings, its markings, the texture of its fur, the glistening of its black lips. He could feel heat – a raging heat that blasted like an open furnace from its mouth as it roared into his face.

No, he was no match for the beast. He couldn't fight it, couldn't outrun it. One wrong move and he and Scooby would be swiped clean off the mountain like a couple of flies.

But there was no going back now, either...

"I've come for my dog," Daniel found himself saying, speaking softly, reassuringly. This was an animal after all – a wild animal, but still an animal, and they responded to kindness, didn't they? "I need to take her home. She's mine. I love her. I have to take care of her."

The beast remained standing over Scooby, slitted yellow eyes fixed on Daniel, beads of saliva dripping from its long fangs.

Slowly, very slowly, Daniel reached out towards his pet, his eyes glued to the beast. "Please, let me have her. You're a spirit, she's alive and she needs me. Let me take her."

The deep yellow feline eyes narrowed, the beast uttered a low, dangerous growl and terror ran through Daniel's veins. It was about to attack, he sensed it. Every nerve in his body warned him. "No! Please don't!" Daniel cried. "Don't hurt us!"

The beast's great gaping jaws opened. Horrific fangs hovered above Daniel's head, ready to snap down on him at any second.

For a moment, time seemed to stand still. Daniel stared helplessly into that black gaping void of the ghostly beast's mouth. Those sabre teeth were deadly, he stood no chance against them.

Scooby rolled in submission onto her back, while below them, Beth screamed.

But Daniel's courage surged back. He wasn't going to simply give in. He wasn't about to be killed by a ghost! Neither was his dog, or Beth, who could easily be its next victim. He wasn't going to roll over and die – at least not without a fight.

A few loose stones littered the ridge, and Daniel snatched one up and held it above his head defiantly as he stared straight into the beast's yellow eyes. "Get back, you monster! I want my dog!"

Karbel's strength was at its peak. The cub would be an easy kill. But he hesitated. What of the human?

Karbel saw the determination in the young male's eyes. He would fight, perhaps to his death. And while this puny human was no match, if Karbel was forced to kill him too, might not his spirit be linked with the cub's? Might he, Karbel, be plagued by the human's spirit throughout eternity?

The thought displeased him immensely. With a mighty roar of frustration, Karbel glanced at the cub baring its belly for the kill – and then he looked at the fearless young male brandishing a stone. Could he kill the cub and have it as his companion for ever without the human interfering? Could he avoid killing the male? Should he risk it?

Karbel pranced uncertainly, snarling in his dilemma.

The risk was great...too great.

He knew suddenly that he couldn't take that chance. A solitary existence was far more desirable than to be cursed with a human for ever.

Let the human take his cub, he would go on as always – alone.

Daniel tried desperately to look fierce, to make out he was a threat to this ghostly apparition. He brandished the stone and quite suddenly – to his amazement – the beast turned tail and leaped up to the ridge above.

Stunned, and barely able to believe his good fortune, Daniel made a grab for Scooby and hauled her down.

Bundling her inside his jacket, he pulled the drawstrings tight. For a second, he savoured the joy of having his pet safely back.

Then Beth yelled from below. "Hurry, Daniel, hurry! The beast is only just above you, it's watching you. It might still come after you!"

With his heart thudding, Daniel lowered himself down from ledge to ledge. It was trickier to descend, especially with Scooby tucked inside his jacket. But he did his best, painstakingly clambering over one rocky ridge to the next one below, ignoring the scrapes and scratches, apologizing to his pet every time he bumped her, or squashed her too tightly. Aware that the beast might come after them at any moment.

Gradually, the rocky ground grew closer. He could see Beth clearly and they could speak to each other without shouting. Finally the softness of moss was underfoot, and Beth's arms were around him.

chapter twelve

"You were so brave, Daniel," Beth gasped as they raced down through the valley. "I really thought the beast was going to kill both of you."

"So did I," Daniel replied, glancing back over his shoulder and praying the beast wasn't playing cat and mouse, and wouldn't come bounding after them at any second.

But they reached the camp safely, and while

Daniel's instant thoughts were to burst in on his dad and blurt out the whole story, he hesitated...

If they told the adults, either they wouldn't be believed, or worse, Melissa would make such a fuss that paranormal investigators would come from far and wide for ever more. Somehow, that just didn't seem right. The beast had existed here for thousands of years and, as far as he knew, it hadn't killed anyone yet. But if hoards of psychic experts came and tracked it down, who knows how it would react. When manifested, it was a vicious, dangerous wild animal.

It could easily have killed him and Scooby. Maybe he had scared it off by waving that stone at it. Yet somehow, he didn't think so. He couldn't have looked very threatening – and deep down he'd been terrified.

He thought back to the moment when he had looked deep into the beast's eyes, just before it had turned away. He had seen a flicker there of... something. He didn't know what it was, but he thought maybe the beast had reasons of its own for not attacking. And he knew he would always be grateful for that.

"Do you think the grown-ups will believe us this time?" Beth whispered as they stood a little way back from the tents.

"Melissa definitely will." He looked steadily at Beth. "But I don't think we should tell them. The beast could have ripped us to pieces, Beth, but it didn't. I don't know why. But if we tell the adults what happened, they won't rest till they've hunted it down. Don't you think we should just leave it in peace? As a little thank-you for it not hurting us or Scooby?"

Beth thought for a second and then nodded. "We'll have to make up a story about Scooby just finding her way back then."

Daniel grinned. "Shouldn't be too difficult."

Creeping into his dad's tent, Daniel placed Scooby on his dad's chest and stood back. His dad instantly woke up and, seeing Scooby standing over him, gave a huge whoop of delight.

"She came back!" exclaimed Andrew, spotting Daniel grinning at him. "I knew she would! All that wandering about in the middle of the night! I knew she wouldn't go far."

"Yep, you were right, Dad. She was waiting right here outside the tent when I woke up."

His dad clambered out of his sleeping bag, swooping the little dog into his arms. "Well that is just fantastic news." He spotted Beth then. "What are you doing up at this time of day anyway? I thought you'd be having a lie-in."

"I heard Scooby snuffling, so I got up," she said, glancing sideways at Daniel.

His dad eyed them both suspiciously. "And you had time to get dressed too – the pair of you..."

"I'll go and tell my dad the good news," Beth announced, before Andrew could ask any more questions. "Let me have Scooby, I want to surprise Dad."

Len was as delighted as Andrew and, when he emerged, he was madly planting kisses on the little dog's head.

Melissa wandered sleepily from her tent. "What's going on? What's all the commotion?"

"Scooby has come back!" Daniel said calmly, watching her reaction.

She looked uncertain. "Well, yes, I knew she would. You should never have run off like that last night. I was frantic."

"Yes, you owe Melissa an apology, young man," said his dad, standing with his arms folded.

Daniel knew he didn't. If anything Melissa owed him and Scooby a huge apology. But he guessed that would never happen. She was never going to admit to using his pet as bait.

Gritting his teeth, he muttered, "Sorry."

His dad raised his eyebrows. "Hardly a sincere apology, Daniel."

"It doesn't matter," Melissa said, looking away. "Besides, I have a report to write on this morning's activities. And wait, I've been making sketches of the battle scenes I heard and witnessed..."

She disappeared back into her tent, emerging with a sketchbook full of pencil drawings.

Everyone was fascinated. She had drawn picture after picture. Horrific scenes of death and mayhem cluttered the pages. Sketches of Highland warriors in tartans, brandishing swords that were as big as them. Faces of *real* people. Or at least they had been real, centuries ago.

"You saw all this?" Daniel breathed incredulously.

"It's exactly as I witnessed it," she murmured.

Daniel glanced at Beth, understanding now why Melissa had sounded so distressed that morning.

"Writing all this up will take me quite some time," she added, speaking directly to Daniel. "I won't have much time for other experiments."

"Not even the beast?" he asked quietly.

She smiled – a secretive smile, meant only for him and Beth. Speaking softly, she whispered, "I think we'll let the beast rest in peace, shall we?"

Daniel's sentiments exactly, and he nodded.

Scooby was snuffling around Melissa's tent, looking for biscuits. Melissa lifted her up, and planted a kiss on the top of her golden head, murmuring, "I'm so sorry, little puppy...so sorry."

Then placing her back in Daniel's arms, she

quietly picked up her sketchpad and disappeared into her tent.

They packed up camp later that morning. Everyone was unusually quiet, all lost in their own thoughts about the past few days. As the others got into the van, Daniel gave Scooby a last little walk before the long drive home. Then, just as they were about to climb into the van, Scooby turned towards the mountain and gave a ferocious little *yap*!

Daniel looked. For a moment he couldn't see anything. And then he spotted it. A shimmering mass of light – but there was no mistaking that huge catlike shape, those long fangs.

He was just about to shout to Beth to look, when he changed his mind. The grown-ups might hear. Instead, he scooped Scooby into his arms and held her close, gazing steadily at the beast.

A moment later, the glistening, barely visible shape turned and sprang into the loch, where it padded through the shallows.

Its movements were light and graceful, although nearby a flock of waterfowl took flight in alarm.

Smiling, Daniel boarded the van and Andrew steered them slowly away from the valley up towards the road.

Not surprisingly, the adults were soon chatting about their trip, but Daniel had a question for them. "Why is it that some spirits remain on earth instead of going on to heaven or the afterlife?"

"Who knows?" Melissa mused. "Perhaps that spirit still has work to do in this life. Perhaps there's another task he has to perform on this earth before he can join his forefathers."

Andrew slowed down to manoeuvre around another vehicle parked in the narrow bumpy lane. It was a roadworks lorry. Two men in yellow jackets were erecting a sign at the side of the road.

Endrith Valley bypass. Work starts October for 26 weeks.

Andrew waved as he steered past. "That's going to cause a pretty big disruption when it starts," he remarked.

"I wonder if it will disturb the ghosts of Endrith Valley?" Beth asked, glancing at Daniel.

An odd little shiver ran through Daniel as he cuddled Scooby closer and murmured, "I wouldn't be at all surprised."